HARD LUCK

A ST. LOUIS MAVERICKS HOCKEY ROMANCE

BRENDA ROTHERT

KAT MIZERA

CHAPTER ONE

Lucy

My first time traveling by bus was probably going to be my last. Not only was it hot, the woman across the aisle from me had taken her socks and shoes off and the man in the seat next to mine had just whipped a container of leftovers out of his backpack.

"Mmm, beef and noodles," he said, scarfing down his first mouthful. "Doesn't even need to be heated up…oh, shit."

The bus had hit a bump, causing him to spill his second bite all over the front of his shirt. As he scooped the noodles up with a paper towel, wadding it up and throwing it to the floor where it landed on my shoe, I closed my eyes. I kept telling myself to just breathe.

The downside was having beef and noodles on one of my new flats, but I had to remember that the upside was much bigger than that.

I was officially more than twenty hours away from Spokane, and I was never going back. Traveling by bus wasn't my first choice, but it was the most low-key way to get out of the hell I inadvertently walked into a couple of months ago.

My bag buzzed with a notification on my phone. When I pulled it out, I saw a message from my older brother.

Sawyer: Hey, my teammate Kon is picking you up at the bus station. Here's his contact info in case you need to reach him.

My stomach sank. It seemed like my intuition about my brother was right. It had been six months since his wife Annie died, and he was struggling to move forward. He'd always been an upbeat person who went out of his way to help others. Most of the time he didn't even answer my calls anymore, and it was unlike him to send someone else to pick me up.

Hopefully he wasn't pissed at me. I hadn't asked him if I could come stay with him for a while; I'd texted him a few days ago that I was coming. Before I started over in a new place, I wanted to make sure my brother was okay. He hadn't just lost Annie; he'd had to watch as cancer destroyed her body and stole her from those who loved her.

Cancer had taken everything it could from my sister-in-law, but she'd never conceded a single shred of her spirit. To the end, she'd been grateful for every moment of life and every person around her. Annie and I had been close. I missed her every day, and even though she wasn't here for me to talk to anymore, I usually knew what she would say if she were.

Go pull Sawyer back into the land of the living. I could almost hear her sweet voice saying the words. *Don't take no for an answer—you know how stubborn he is.*

"Hey, you got a knife by chance?" the man next to me asked.

I shook my head.

"Not like a *knife* knife," he said. "They searched our bags so I know no one's got a real one. But like a butter knife? Just something that can cut this?"

He held up a thick slice of ham and I didn't know whether to laugh or cry. My seatmate was basically pulling a Thanksgiving spread out of his backpack.

"Sorry, I've got nothing," I said.

With a shrug, he bit a chunk off the ham. I looked away, grateful that I was changing buses in Chicago.

From there, it was just a few more hours to my final destination—St. Louis.

I was looking forward to seeing my brother and dreading it in equal measure. It would be the first time I'd seen him since Annie's funeral.

The week I'd spent at Sawyer's then had been the hardest of my life. It broke my heart to see him grieving for Annie. My strong brother had been brought to his knees and there was nothing I could do about it. When I'd left him to return to Spokane, I'd assumed he'd slowly get better.

Maybe I was wrong, and he was doing better than I thought. Nothing would make me happier.

What he didn't know, and I wasn't yet ready to tell him, was that this might be the last time we saw each other for a long time.

I'd closed out my bank account and sold everything I owned in Spokane, including my car. When I left St. Louis, I was starting over somewhere new. Somewhere quiet and out of the way. Somewhere I hoped I'd be safe.

———

"Have you been to the Lou before?" the guy next to me for the Chicago to St. Louis bus ride asked.

He seemed nice enough, and he wasn't tossing food onto my shoes, so I smiled and responded.

"A few times. My brother lives there."

"Cool. I was visiting a buddy at the University of Chicago and now I'm heading back to school. St. Louis University. I'm Sam."

"Hey Sam. I'm Lucy."

Instinct made me keep my voice down. Even though I knew no one on this bus was following me, I carried fear around like a heavy package I couldn't put down. It was always there, even when I tried to reason my way out of it.

I'd be safe at Sawyer's. I just had to get there. If he knew who and what I was running from, I knew he would have come to pick me up himself. I couldn't blame him for sending a teammate, though, because I hadn't told him yet.

Shame was a lot like grief. It didn't come from a logical place, and it was hard to send it packing. I felt shame for the situation I was in, whether I'd knowingly walked into it or not.

"How old are you, Lucy?" Sam asked.

"I'm twenty-seven."

He grinned. "Well, I like older women. Some buddies are picking me up at the bus station and we're going out. I'd love for you to join us."

I laughed, and Sam's expression turned sober.

"No, I'm laughing because it's been a hot second since anyone asked me out," I said.

Sam grinned. "Why? You're superhot."

"With no makeup? In my hoodie?" This was going from funny to hilarious.

"Hell yeah."

"You're sweet, but someone's picking me up at the bus station."

Sam drew his brows together. "Your boyfriend?"

"No."

"Do you have a boyfriend?"

"Uh...not really." Before he could say another word, I added, "But I did twenty-four hours ago."

Sam's whole face lit up. "So you're on the rebound? I'm a perfect rebound guy. We can party that asshole all the way out of your system, Lucy."

He did a little dance from the waist up and I responded with a polite smile.

"I appreciate the offer, but I'm just going to catch up with my brother tonight."

With a shrug, he turned his attention to his phone. Apparently, I wasn't worth talking to since I didn't want to go out with him.

When the bus finally slowed to a stop at the terminal, I exhaled hard, glad to have reached the end of my journey.

My phone vibrated with a text and I looked

down at the screen. It was from an unknown number.

Unknown: Hi Lucy, this is Konstantin. I am here to pick you up. I'm waiting in the terminal. Dark hair. Gray shirt. Many tats.

I vaguely remembered meeting him at Annie's funeral. His suit had been a stark contrast to the ink on his neck. He seemed kind of intense—the opposite of Sawyer's happy-go-lucky, extroverted teammate Nash.

Nash was funny and sweet. Why couldn't Sawyer have sent *him* to pick me up?

I responded to the text.

Lucy: Hi, the bus just arrived. I'll be there soon. Thanks for coming to get me.

Unknown: No prob.

People were starting to file off the bus, so I stood, my phone buzzing with another text as I waited for my turn.

Nate: Where the hell are you?

Nate: I called the spa you said you were going to. You lying bitch.

My heart pounded in my chest and I grabbed the top of the seat in front of me, feeling light-headed. I knew this was coming. I sold or left behind everything to my name except the clothes in the two bags I'd brought on the bus and my phone.

I needed to be able to reach Sawyer in case my travel plans changed, and I'd considered getting a burner cell phone, but that seemed too *Jason Bourne.* It didn't anymore.

He was going to find me. I knew that. All I wanted was to be safely at Sawyer's before he did. And even though he was probably still in Spokane, his texts spooked me. I felt like he could see me right now, like he could grab me at any moment.

Nate: You can't hide from me. My brother will find you.

I stepped into the aisle of the bus, the line moving slowly. My grip on the small bag I'd carried onto the bus was so tight my hand burned.

As soon as I reached the bus stairs, I rushed down them and gulped in fresh air, forcing myself not to look at the texts that were hitting my phone in rapid-fire succession. I powered it off and shoved it into my pocket.

Walking around to the back of the bus, I passed the driver, who was opening the door to the baggage compartment. This was my chance, and I had to take it. I walked to the other side of the bus and took my phone out of my pocket.

After looking over both shoulders to make sure no one could see me, I quickly wedged the phone under the huge tire of the bus. Nate would find me eventually, but he would never terrorize me by phone again. Knowing the bus would crush the phone—and those unread texts—gave me a small thrill.

With a deep breath, I walked around to get my other bag from the bus driver. I put the straps of both bags over my shoulders and headed for the terminal.

I saw Konstantin as soon as I walked in. He was hard to miss. Tall and lean, he had inked arms and short, dark stubble coating his cheeks.

"Hey, Kon," I said, forcing myself to smile even though I still felt sick from Nate's texts.

"Lucy." He nodded, not smiling. "I'll take your bags."

"Oh, you don't need to"

"Give them to me." His voice was gruff.

I wasn't in the mood to argue about anything, least of all who was going to carry my bags. I just wanted to get the hell out of there, and fast.

"How was your trip here?" Kon asked as he took my bags.

"Fine," I said. "But I accidentally left my phone on the bus."

He turned to me, his brow furrowed. "We should let someone know, so they can return it if someone turns it in."

He had a distinct accent, though I had no trouble understanding him.

I waved a hand. "No, I'm not worried about it. It was an old phone anyway. I'd rather just start fresh and get a new one."

"Okay."

I fell into step beside him. "Hey, how's my brother doing?"

He was silent.

"That good, huh?" I cracked.

"You will see."

CHAPTER TWO

Kon

It was rare to have a full day off during hockey season, so the last thing I wanted to do was get dressed and drive thirty minutes to pick someone up from the bus terminal. My friend and teammate, Sawyer, had been the one to ask, though, and I didn't have it in me to say no. The last couple years of my life had been a shit show, but his had been a million times worse. Watching him slowly lose his wife to cancer had been hard and watching what had happened to him since was even harder.

The whole team had rallied around Sawyer, willing to do almost anything to alleviate some of his suffering, but nothing worked. If anything, the more we tried, the more we pissed him off. So I sure as shit wasn't going to refuse when he'd reached out and asked me to pick up his sister, Lucy.

I'd briefly met her at Annie's funeral. What a fucked-up day that had been. I was pretty sure no one liked funerals, but that one had been gut wrenching. I was Russian and had been taught at an early age to keep my emotions in check, but two funerals in two years had been a lot. We'd lost our team captain and his wife the year before in a car accident, so it felt like a lot of grief for such a small group.

"Kon?"

With a start, I realized Lucy had been talking to me and I glanced over at her apologetically.

"I'm sorry. What did you say?"

"Could we stop at the grocery store? I was thinking I'd make dinner tonight. I'm willing to bet Sawyer hasn't eaten a decent meal in a while."

I nodded. "This is probably correct. Yes, we can stop. There is a store close to the house."

"Thanks." She paused. "I hope I didn't take you away from anything important today."

"No. Usually I rest on days off."

"I'm sorry to disrupt your routine." She hesitated, as if something was on her mind. "Do you know why Sawyer couldn't come get me?"

I blew out a breath, unsure how much to tell her. She was here, so she was going to see for herself what was going on with her brother. I hated throwing my buddy under the bus, but his behavior lately hadn't been pretty and I didn't know how much longer he could continue down the path he was on.

"I am not sure," I said carefully.

She made a face. "Annie had a feeling he was going to spiral, so she made me promise I'd keep an eye on him. I meant to come sooner, but I had some things to deal with at home before I could get away."

"You live in Seattle?"

"No, Spokane. Well, not anymore."

"No? You will move here?" I asked curiously.

"I don't know yet. If I can get Sawyer squared away, I'm thinking about going on an adventure." She grinned over at me almost shyly, and I couldn't help but smile back.

"What kind of adventure?"

"I haven't decided yet."

"Sounds interesting."

"We'll see."

The momentary mischief on her face was cute but there was something in her eyes that was wary too, as if there was more to the story. Not that it was any of my business.

"What about your boyfriend?" I remembered a stocky guy who was losing his hair that had been with her at the funeral. "Is he going to move with you?"

She lifted her chin a fraction. "I ended it before I left. That's partly why I waited until now to come back to St. Louis. I needed to…make a clean break."

I wasn't sure how to respond to that. Luckily, I'd just pulled up to the local grocery store and we made our way inside. She grabbed a cart and made a right toward the produce department. "Would you like to have dinner with us tonight?" she asked over her shoulder. "My way of saying thank you for picking me up."

I should have said no, but the lure of a home-cooked meal was strong. I lived on protein shakes, protein bars, and the precooked meals I had delivered when I wasn't on the road. I'd never learned to cook and my last girlfriend had moved out over a year ago.

"Thank you," I said, following her as she scanned the displays of fresh fruits and vegetables. "It is rare someone cooks for me."

"I love to cook," she said, carefully examining a bin of tomatoes.

"And I love to eat."

"Do you like chicken and dumplings?"

I hesitated. "I...don't know. I do not think I've eaten this before."

"Oh, it's my specialty. Comfort food."

"Comfort food?" My English had come a long way in the last two years, but some phrases didn't translate as well as others.

"You know...food you eat that makes you happy. Like when you're sick and your mother makes a special soup, or something warm and filling when it's cold outside."

"I see." I understood the concept but there had been no such thing growing up in Russia, especially once I started playing hockey. I ate what they put in front of me, whether it comforted me or not.

"Sawyer loves my chicken and dumplings," she continued, putting a ten-pound bag of potatoes in the cart. "I'm trying to think of all his favorite dishes."

"I am sure I will enjoy anything you make," I said, watching her grab a big bag of apples. "What will you make with so many apples?"

She laughed, her sapphire eyes crinkling at the corners. "Pie, cobbler, maybe even an apple spice cake. There are so many options."

"Apple spice..." My voice trailed off. "We do not have desserts like this in Russia."

She bent over to scoop up a runaway orange,

giving me a peek at a shapely little ass hiding beneath the nondescript pants she wore.

Shit.

I'd been doing my best not to notice her bright blue eyes.

Or the full, naturally red lips that didn't need lipstick to stand out.

Definitely not the tits that bounced as she walked.

Nope. I wasn't going there.

The last thing I needed was to start something with a woman who was leaving.

Even a beautiful one who'd recently become single.

I PARKED my SUV on the street in front of Sawyer's townhouse and hit the button to open the hatch in the back. Between Lucy's luggage and over four hundred dollars worth of groceries, it would take a few trips to get everything inside, so I told Lucy to go ahead while I grabbed her two suitcases.

"I'll bring everything in," I said, motioning toward the front door. "Do you have a key?"

"Yeah." She pulled a small key chain out of her purse and I followed her up the walkway.

She rang the bell before putting the key in the lock and opening the door.

"Sawyer? It's me!"

We stepped inside and I grimaced as the smell of stale beer and urine hit me. What the hell was going on in here? I'd known he was spiraling, but I hadn't expected this level of filth.

"Jesus." Lucy stopped so abruptly I almost ran into her.

The house looked like a tornado had plowed through it. There were half-eaten containers of food littering almost every flat surface, empty beer bottles on the floor and coffee table, and a stack of unopened mail that was at least eight or ten inches thick sat on the floor of the foyer. The TV was on, the volume at an alarming level, and I looked around for the remote as we walked into the living room.

I spotted Sawyer, passed out in the armchair by the window, and he looked even worse than the last time I'd seen him, which said something.

I turned off the TV as Lucy crossed the room and leaned over her brother, shaking his shoulder. "Sawyer! Hey, wake up."

He started, slowly opening bloodshot eyes. He frowned for a second before sitting up. "Oh. Hey. When did you get here?" His words were slightly slurred.

"Just now." She leaned over, giving him a one-armed hug. "I've missed you."

"I missed you too." He awkwardly patted her shoulder. He hadn't shaved in a while, and his hair looked greasy, as if it hadn't been washed in a long time. Hell, based on the body odor I got a whiff of, he hadn't even been showering.

She straightened up and slowly looked around, as if taking it all in. To her credit, she didn't react, merely turned back to him. "We, uh, got groceries. Are you hungry?"

He shrugged, scratching his chin. "I could eat, I guess."

"You want to take a shower while I put the groceries away and make dinner?"

He hesitated. "I'm kinda tired, Luce."

"A shower will make you feel better." She nudged him before turning to me. "Kon, would you mind getting the groceries out of the car?"

"Sure." I turned and went outside, thinking she was stronger than a lot of women might be under the circumstances. I wasn't sure I could have been so patient had he been my brother, but of course, we were guys so our dynamic would have been different.

I grabbed as many plastic grocery bags as I could carry and brought them into the house. Sawyer was still in the chair and Lucy had squatted down next to him, talking in a soft voice. Not wanting to intrude, I made two more trips out to the car, bringing everything in and putting it all in the kitchen. If she hadn't invited me to dinner, I would have made a hasty escape, but I hated leaving her to deal with this on her own. It wasn't just Sawyer that was a mess, but the house was a pigsty. It didn't look this bad the last time I'd been here.

Impulsively, I dug around in the pantry until I found a box of garbage bags. I grabbed one and brought it with me into the living room. Sawyer was stumbling his way up the stairs and there was no doubt Lucy was struggling with whether or not to help him.

"Let him do it on his own," I said quietly.

She nodded, absently taking the bag from me and began picking up some of the garbage. We worked together, gathering old pizza boxes, beer bottles, and Styrofoam cups.

"Apparently, he fired his cleaning lady. I need to get in touch with her because this place is a disaster."

"What can I do to help?" I asked.

"You've done plenty," she said, giving me a tight smile. "I'll figure out what's next. I just hadn't realized..." Her voice trailed. "Did you know he had fallen this low?"

"No." I felt like shit about it, too. I was going to have to mention this to my teammates.

"Would you mind if we had dinner another night? I can't even imagine cooking in that kitchen right now. I'm sorry I—"

"It's okay." I put a hand on her shoulder, cutting her off. "Don't worry about me. Do what you have to do."

"Thank you."

"Sawyer has my number. You can use his phone to text me if you need anything. I mean it. This is a lot."

"We'll be fine, but I appreciate the offer. And I will text you. As soon as I whip this place into shape." Her smile, despite everything going on, was genuine. "I owe you chicken and dumplings."

"You owe me nothing." I gently squeezed her shoulder, wishing there was more I could do. "We leave for a road trip tomorrow, but we'll be back Tuesday."

"Don't worry about us." She glanced in the direction Sawyer had gone. "Thanks for being here, though. And thanks for being his friend."

I didn't know why she was thanking me; it felt like we had all failed Sawyer in the friend department.

CHAPTER THREE

Lucy

THE SOUND of a news broadcaster on a TV got louder as I walked downstairs. Apparently, the long bus trip here had worn me out; I'd slept until nine fifteen this morning. Hopefully Sawyer already had a pot of coffee on.

My heart sank as I walked into the main family room, where the blinds were still closed and he was asleep on the couch, empty beer cans littering the coffee table. It wasn't that Sawyer was up and listening to the news; he'd never left the couch last night.

When I looked at his peaceful expression, tears welled in my eyes. I could still see the round-cheeked, smiling little boy he'd been. We'd fought as kids, like most siblings, but if anyone else picked on me, my big brother had jumped in to defend me every time.

It was me who wanted to protect him now, but I couldn't. Not only had his wife died, he'd also had to watch her slowly deteriorate. And now he still woke up every day in the house they'd picked out together when they moved here, the bed they'd slept inthat she'd died inlikely haunting him.

I went into the kitchen and found what I needed to start a pot of coffee, then opened all the blinds on the main level of the house and resumed the cleaning Kon and I had started yesterday evening.

"What the hell?" Sawyer grumbled as I tossed his empty beer cans into a trash bag. "What's going on?"

"Just cleaning things up."

He raised his head from the couch a few notches, then dropped it back down immediately.

"No, you don't need to do that."

"Are you planning to just buy another coffee table when this one's covered with beer cans?" I cracked.

"Stop yelling, Luce. I'm trying to sleep."

I shook my head as he scowled, his eyes still closed. Things with him were a lot worse than I'd imagined. When he didn't return to his team at the start of the new season, I worried he might be depressed.

It was obvious he was in a bad place, and I had to help him find a way out. I didn't know if he needed tough love or lots of encouragement, though. Part of me wanted to tell him to get his ass in gear and another part wanted to eat ice cream and watch movies with him.

My gaze wandered to the wall behind the couch. When I came for Annie's funeral, photos from their wedding and vacations they'd taken had hung there. I remembered one in particular of them standing in front of a waterfall in Hawaii, looking happy and full of life. Now the wall was empty, which tore me to pieces.

I didn't know what to do, so I went into the kitchen and started prep work for the beef stew I was making for dinner tonight. After searching the kitchen cabinets, I found the slow cooker in the walk-in pantry on a shelf, its cord neatly wrapped into a bundle.

Annie. She'd been gone for six months, but she was still here in so many ways. I had no right feeling sorry for myself over what had gone down with Nate; my brother was living through a heartbreaking reality that felt like a nightmare.

Kon and I had gotten through all the dishes

yesterday, but there was so much cleaning left to do that I'd decided to make dinner in the slow cooker and throw myself into cleaning today.

First order of business—the bathroom I was using. It was coated in dust and had a stale, closed-up smell. It took me almost two hours to clean it from top to bottom, and I was drenched in sweat by the time I finished. Not to mention bored as hell.

"Hey, sleepyhead," I said to Sawyer, who was snoring on the couch. "Can I use your phone?"

"What?" He squinted at me. "Lucy?"

"Yep. It's almost noon. Time to get up and moving."

He groaned. "What have you been doing, running?"

"Cleaning."

Another groan. "No. I don't want you coming in here and messing shit up, Luce."

I laughed, crossing my arms. "You think I messed up the dark rings in the toilet?"

He sat up and rubbed his temple, then fished around in the couch cushions for his phone. When he found it, he took one look at the screen and gave me a confused look.

"What the hell? Nate's blowing up my phone. He hasn't called or texted me this much in the whole time you guys have dated. What's going on with you two?"

My heart raced as he looked at me expectantly. What was going on was too much to condense into a couple of sentences.

"There's nothing going on," I said shortly. "I broke it off and he's not happy about it."

"Well, why the fuck isn't he just blowing up your phone? What's it got to do with me?"

There were so many things I didn't like about my brother right now. His tone, his attitude, and his beard were at the top of the list.

"I lost my phone on the trip here," I lied. "And I didn't tell him where I was going, so he's probably looking for me."

Sawyer rubbed his brow. "I don't...why didn't you tell him where you were going?"

He got up from the couch and walked into the kitchen, and I followed.

"We broke up," I reminded him. "Meaning, we're over and we no longer tell each other where we're going."

He opened a kitchen cabinet and grabbed a bottle of Tylenol. Apparently drinking an entire case of beer in a short period of time gave him a headache. Shocker.

"Don't you work at his insurance office, though?"

he asked as he shook a couple of pills into his hand. "Or did you quit?"

"I quit."

He popped the pills into his mouth and walked over to the sink to get a glass of water. After drinking it, he turned to face me, leaning back against the kitchen counter.

"Do you want to talk about it?" he asked.

I looked away. "Not right now. Just trust me that I made the right decision."

He nodded. "You want me to tell him to back the fuck off?"

"Maybe? I don't know. I don't want him to know where I am, but he'll find me eventually, so…I don't know."

"Find you?" Sawyer's brow was furrowed with concern. "Luce, if he comes here looking for you and you don't want to see him, I'll send his ass packing."

Tears flooded my eyes, clouding my vision. Despite everything that was going on with him, Sawyer was still looking out for me like he always had. I was relieved to be here, where I felt safer than I had in a long time.

"I don't want to see him."

He took a few steps closer to me, examining my face. "Why are you crying? Did he hurt you? If he put a hand on you, I'm not waiting for him to show up here. I'll be on the next flight to Spokane."

I smiled. He didn't seem to be in any condition to kick ass, but maybe his devil-may-care attitude meant he was in the perfect condition for it.

"I want to leave everything about him behind," I said. "I just want to be here with you."

He sighed heavily. "That was a nonanswer. So yes, he did hurt you."

"Not physically."

He arched a brow, skeptical.

"He didn't," I said. "I promise. But he did threaten to, and I think he would have if I'd stayed."

"He's welcome to come try," he said, narrowing his eyes. "I've got nothing to lose."

"I don't agree with you there." I walked over to the small kitchen nook and pulled out a chair. "Why don't you sit down and I'll make some coffee and breakfast and we can talk?"

He scoffed. "I'm not hungry."

"Well, I am." I walked over to the refrigerator and took out the carton of eggs I'd bought.

"What's all that?" Sawyer asked, peering at the fridge full of groceries.

"Kon took me to the grocery store on the way here yesterday."

He groaned. "And then you did my dishes."

"With Kon's help."

That really seemed to set him off. He threw his hands in the air and glared at me.

"Look, if you want to stay here, you can, but I don't need you or anyone else cleaning my house and buying me food. He's my fucking teammate, not my nanny."

I glared back at him. "You had nothing but mustard, bologna, and beer in your fridge."

"Yeah," he shot back. "You squirt some mustard on the bologna and roll it up and eat it. Wash it down with the beer. Sorry I don't have any beef bourguignon for you."

I rolled my eyes. "There's a lot of room between expired bologna and beef bourguignon, Sawyer."

"My bologna is not expired," he said indignantly.

"It expired two weeks ago, which is why it went in the trash."

He gave me a disgusted look as he walked over to the fridge, opened the door, and looked inside.

"You threw away my bologna." He shook his head. "Or was it Kon? That douchebag probably ate it."

I laughed at the absurdity of it. "No one wanted to eat your expired bologna. I threw it away."

Sawyer pulled a can of beer from the refrigerator, popped the top and took a sip.

"Don't throw my shit away," he said. "And don't clean my house. I own it. I'll decide how clean it is."

I just stared at him, stunned. It wasn't even afternoon yet and he was already hitting the booze. Did he do this every day?

"Is this working for you?" I asked him.

"What?"

I gestured at nothing and everything all at once. "You know…beer, bologna, and toilet rings. Hangovers. Not playing hockey."

He took another drink of the beer and then sneered at me. "Listen, Luce, if you came here to get all high and mighty and judge me, you can turn around and walk right back out the door."

"Is that what you want me to do?"

He considered. "Maybe not today because of this Nate thing. But if you're going to be here, respect that this is *my* house. My life. My choices."

His house, life, and choices were all a disaster at the moment, but I decided to back down. I'd have to take things slowly. Make him think eating something other than bologna was his idea.

"I'll respect that," I said. "Is it okay if I cook and clean a few things to keep my mind occupied? I don't have anything else to do."

He waved a hand. "Yeah, whatever."

"And can I use your phone for music while I

clean? And to text Kon and find a cell phone store so I can go buy a new one?"

He went into the family room, grabbed his phone, and passed it to me. "You can use my car, too. Keys are on the hook by the garage."

"Thanks."

"Why do you need to text Kon?" he asked me.

"To invite him over for dinner."

He shook his head. "You don't need to do that. Kon's a moody bastard."

"I already invited him, actually. I just need to tell him a time."

Sawyer grunted in response, grabbing another can of beer from the fridge and walking back into the family room. "Tell that fucker he owes me a package of bologna."

I gave his retreating form a wry look. "I'll be sure to do that."

CHAPTER FOUR

Kon

I HAD a love-hate relationship with road trips. While I loved the hockey elements and hanging out with my teammates in small doses, being on top of each other every day wore on my introverted soul. I preferred the peace and quiet of my apartment, my king-size bed, and not having to think of things to talk about. While my English had gotten much better since I'd moved to St. Louis, it was still my second language, which meant I struggled sometimes.

Today was one of those days that made me want to run screaming from the room. My buddy Michael Boone was thinking about asking his girlfriend to marry him, so he was all about engagement rings and getting ideas for romantic ways to propose. Thankfully, I had no experience with either so no one was looking to me for information, but there was nowhere for me to escape on the plane.

"I think private is best," Lars Janssen said. The burly Swedish D-man had gotten married this past summer after proposing to his wife on Valentine's Day.

"Yeah, that way you have an out if she says no," Rory Beauchamp, another D-man, quipped.

"Thanks a lot!" Boone laughed, raising his middle finger in the air.

"I agree that the proposal should be private," our team captain, Wes Kirby, chimed in. "The engagement part, wedding, all of that is a big deal, but the proposal should be just the two of you. Maybe a photographer if you feel the need to capture the moment for all eternity." He grinned even as he rolled his eyes.

"I don't care about all that," Boone mused, "but *she* might. I want to make this all about her, you know?"

"Are you sure she's the one?" Nash asked, frowning. "Didn't you guys have a big blowout over the summer?"

"We worked it out and I'm trying to show her I'm all in."

"Kinda hard to do with a micropeen like yours," Rory said dryly.

"You wish you had a peen like mine," Boone shot back.

"Just do what feels right to you," Wes said, ignoring them. "You know her better than we do."

The conversation went on around me and I tried to tune them out without being rude. After our goalie had retired at the end of last season, I'd taken over his starting position, which required a bit of locker-room leadership. Not like what the captain did, but a more subtle way of guiding them when necessary.

My teammates were great guys, which I appreciated. I was a bit closer to Boone and Sawyer than the others, though Sawyer and I obviously hadn't had much of a relationship lately. I would have been lying if I said I hadn't missed his friendship the last few months. Boone was my party buddy, but Sawyer had been my more serious friend. Someone I felt comfortable just hanging out with. No pressure to be smart or funny. I could just *be*.

Annie and I had been friends too. She'd been learning a little Russian, determined to make me feel more comfortable when we hung out, and I missed her hilarious texts asking me how to pronounce curse words. The best ones—and I'd saved them all because they still made me smile—were her voice texts. Her mispronounced "fuck you" had me rolling at one point.

"Anyone new in your life these days?" Boone asked when the proposal chatter had settled down. "That redhead at The Crazy Horse was hot."

I shrugged. "Was just a lap dance. Nothing more." I had no problem with strippers, but I wasn't in the market for anything beyond sex. Not with a stripper or anyone else.

"You can't pout over Svetlana forever, dude."

The mention of my lying, cheating ex made me scowl.

"Don't," I warned.

I hated talking about her. I'd been humiliated when she didn't just cheat on me, but did it behind my back with a former teammate. On top of that, I hadn't ended things right away. We had a shared past. She'd been with me through some of the darkest days of my life, so I'd fought to save the relationship. I initially couldn't wrap my head around the idea of being without her, though I'd eventually done what needed to be done.

The whole thing had soured me on relationships and aside from a healthy dose of casual hookups, always on the road, I'd steered clear of anything even vaguely resembling a relationship ever since.

My thoughts inadvertently strayed to a pair of big blue eyes, and I realized I'd thought of Lucy several times over the last few days. I wondered how she was, if Sawyer was making her life hell, or if she needed anything. I hadn't heard from her, so I figured she was okay, but it reminded me to mention the situation to Wes.

"Hey." I leaned forward and tapped his shoulder.

"What's up?" He turned curiously.

"I saw Sawyer the other day."

"Yeah?" He unbuckled his seat belt and turned to the side so we could talk more easily. "How is he?"

I shook my head. "Bad. Worse than ever."

He made a face. "Really?"

"His sister came to town and I had to pick her up from the bus terminal because he was passed out drunk."

Wes sighed, looking away. We all understood grief, and while Sawyer's may have been a little more poignant, it was time for him to at least try to return to the land of the living. His spiral into a cycle of grief and despair wasn't healthy.

"He has to deal with this in his own time," Lars said patiently. "You cannot rush grief."

"This is more than that," I said. "He's not showering, not eating, not doing anything but drinking. The house was…a mess."

"Might be time for us to be a little more proactive," Wes said. "I think we all need to check in more regularly. Let me think about it and maybe I can come up with a plan."

I agreed we needed to do something; I just wasn't sure what could be done.

I wanted to help my friend, but he had to be willing to accept help.

And from what I'd seen, he wasn't.

AFTER BACK-TO-BACK WINS in Atlanta and North Carolina, I was in a good mood on the flight home. My teammates were as rowdy and obnoxious as ever, making me laugh despite how annoying they were. A few of the guys were going out after we landed, but I was ready to sleep in my own bed. I wasn't much of a partier in general, and after spending the last week with my teammates every minute we weren't sleeping, it would be good to just chill.

I was playing a game on my phone when an unfamiliar number popped up with a text.

Unknown: Hi, Kon. This is Lucy. I finally got a new

phone.

Kon: Hello! How are things with Sawyer?

Lucy: Ugh. You don't want to know.

Kon: Still bad?

Lucy: Well, I guess it depends on how you define bad. The cleaning service is coming once a week again, so the house is in good shape. I've also got Sawyer eating at least one meal a day, so that's an improvement. Beyond that...

Kon: Is there anything I can do?

Lucy: I don't know. He's worse than I imagined, and I don't want to push him. You know how stubborn he is. The more we push, the harder he'll push back.

Kon: I'm sorry. The guys on the team are going to try to visit more. Even if he doesn't want us to.

Lucy: That's a good idea. Just warn them he won't be overly friendly.

Kon: He was never overly friendly to begin with.

Lucy: You didn't know Sawyer before Annie got sick. Anyway, the real reason I texted was to invite you to that dinner I promised you.

Kon: It's not necessary. You have enough going on without having guests.

Lucy: But I love to cook and having someone else here to engage with Sawyer is the only thing I can think of that might help. Maybe not right away, but if we do it consistently enough maybe something will break through.

Kon: Then I would love to come.

Lucy: You get back tonight and have a game tomorrow, so how about Thursday? Does that work for you? I don't know if you have meetings or other plans?

Kon: Probably practice in the morning, but nothing the rest of the day. Tell me what time and what kind of wine to bring.

Lucy: I'm making chicken and dumplings, as promised, so how about a white?

Kon: Chardonnay or Chablis?

Lucy: Surprise me.

Kon: I don't know much about wine.

Lucy: Whatever looks good to you. I really like Napa Valley wineries.

Kon: Okay.

Lucy: Six o'clock? We eat pretty early these days.

Kon: Six is perfect. I eat early as well.

Lucy: See you soon.

Kon: I'm looking forward to it.

Lucy: Me too.

I put my phone away and realized I was looking forward to seeing her again. I wasn't sure why because there was nothing between us, but I felt a pull. Dealing with Sawyer's situation on the back end of what I assumed was an unpleasant breakup had to be draining. I wanted to be there for her, even if for no other reason than to lend a friendly shoulder for her to lean on. My gut told me she didn't have a lot of people she could rely on in her life, and I felt that deep in my soul. Other than my teammates, and the grandmother who'd raised me in Russia, I had no one.

I'd lost my parents at a young age. My mother's mother had raised me, but we'd had less than nothing. I went to bed cold and hungry more nights than not, and if it hadn't been for the hockey program the local church had offered, I probably wouldn't have survived. Even then, I'd only had one meal a day and I'd tried to save something for my grandmother. Half a piece of bread, leftover broth, anything to keep her going. It had been that bad.

I shook off the depressing thoughts.

I'd fought my way out of hell both literally and figuratively, and while Lucy's situation was nothing like mine, the cold, hungry little boy I'd been always wanted to help someone in need. Sometimes it was as much of a curse as it was a blessing, but I couldn't seem to help myself.

I'd just restarted the game on my phone when another text popped up.

Svetlana: Konstantin, are you there? I really need to talk to you. Please call me.

Jesus. Fucking. Christ.

What fresh hell was this?

Last I'd heard, she was going back to Russia.

Nope.

I wasn't getting involved, no matter what mess she'd gotten herself into.

Not my circus, not my monkeys.

I deleted the text and turned off my phone.

CHAPTER FIVE

Lucy

SAWYER HADN'T EVEN GOTTEN the refrigerator door all the way open when I came over and gently closed it.

"Hey, before you do that, I need you to pick up a couple of things from the store."

He cringed, then looked relieved as he reached for the fridge handle again. "I'll just order from DoorDash. My guy Jimmy's got us."

"You have a DoorDash guy? Like a regular one?"

He shrugged. "He usually brings my orders. I'm a good tipper so we're friendly."

"Okay, so that's good, but...when was the last time you left this house?"

"I have no idea, ballbuster. Will you move your hand?"

I slid in front of the refrigerator, my back against the door so he couldn't open it. I didn't want him reaching for his first beer of the day at only eleven in the morning.

He had a routine, sad as it was. Every day he woke up on the couch, immediately took two Tylenol and drank half a cup of the coffee I'd left in the pot. Then a quick pee, and after that he cracked open his first canned Budweiser of the day.

The first of at least fifteen, from what I could tell. And it definitely showed—he had a thicker waistline than I'd ever seen on him. At this rate, he wouldn't be able to return to the Mavericks even if he wanted to, though as of now, he most definitely didn't.

"I'm particular about my groceries," I said. "I only like certain brands, and one of the things I need is tomatoes. I don't want Jimmy bringing bad tomatoes that'll ruin the salad."

He let out a groan of frustration. "Fuck salads, Luce."

I didn't mention that he needed more salads and a lot less beer if he ever wanted to play pro hockey again. He spent his afternoons watching old games on TV, some from decades ago and others that he played in recently. That told me his love for the game was still there, even if it was buried deep beneath his sadness right now.

"Can you just pick up these things?" I passed him the list I'd handwritten.

He took it and read, glancing up at me with a furrowed brow. "Sweetened condensed milk? I don't even know what that is, let alone where to find it."

"In the baking aisle. It's for the dessert I'm making."

Blondie brownies with ice cream and caramel had been an early morning brainstorm a few hours ago, when I was sitting out on Sawyer's patio, a blanket wrapped around me as I sipped my morning coffee and tried to think of ways to get him to leave the house.

"That's what the ice cream is for, too?" he asked.

He loved ice cream. I was pretty much a genius.

"Yes."

"Breyer's homemade vanilla *only*," he read from the list, giving me a look. "Which is bullshit because it's not homemade."

"It's the best, though. You'll love it. And I'm making homemade caramel to put on the ice cream."

He sighed heavily. "This shopping list is going to take me like an hour."

Like he had other plans? I knew my brother, and I could get him to do what I wanted, but I had to hold back my snarky comments and make him think he was doing me a huge favor.

"I really appreciate it," I said, stepping away from the refrigerator door. "Did Mom call you this morning?"

He shrugged. "Haven't looked at my phone yet."

"She left me a message earlier and said she was going to call you. While you're at the store, I'll call her and check in for both of us."

That sealed the deal. I saw the moment his expression shifted from *probably* to *definitely*. My brother wasn't a fan of phone conversations, and our mother could talk for days.

"Okay, I'll go get your stuff."

"Thanks. Kon said he's bringing a bottle of wine."

Sawyer scoffed. "Guarantee he's never tasted wine in his life. I've got some good vodka he gave me for Christmas last year. He and I will get into that."

I sighed to myself. Was getting drunk with someone else progress from getting drunk alone? If so, it wasn't much.

I'd told Mom over the phone this morning that Sawyer was down, but I hadn't let on how bad it really was. She'd relocated to Scottsdale to care for her sister, who had Alzheimer's. I didn't want her worrying about Sawyer when she already had her hands full.

Somehow, I'd figure this out. I had to. I couldn't stay here indefinitely, and I wasn't leaving until I knew my brother was back on his feet.

———

Kon's expression when he took his first bite of the blondie brownies I'd made with ice cream and caramel drizzle said more than words ever could. Wide eyes and a slight slump of his shoulders—he was a fan.

"I love this," he said, immediately scooping up a second bite.

He and Sawyer demolished the chicken and dumplings and mashed potatoes I'd made, both devouring two huge platefuls. Watching them enjoy food I had cooked was the best feeling I'd had in a long time. Things with Nate had been so tense, and at times, scary, that cooking was the last thing on my mind.

"This is amazing, Luce," Sawyer said.

"Thanks."

He'd eaten more tonight than I'd seen him eat since I arrived last week. And he and Kon had talked hockey while I finished cooking earlier, the sound of them laughing together making me content.

I was so full from dinner that I was very slowly

eating my dessert. My eyes met Kon's across the table, his gaze dark and intense even now. If I didn't know he was such a nice guy, that gaze would have intimidated me. I thought I saw fearlessness and strength there, a calm that could turn into a storm when needed.

Glancing down, I was flooded with self-doubt. I no longer trusted myself to judge someone's character after I'd so completely misjudged Nate.

I'd fallen for his trusted hometown insurance agent persona just like so many other people had. As his office manager and girlfriend, though, I should have figured out sooner that he wasn't who he was pretending to be. That mistake had been a costly one.

"Do you like the wine?" Kon asked me.

"Yes, it's very good."

I'd only drank one glass because I wasn't a heavy drinker. And as Sawyer had predicted, Kon hadn't had any. He'd gotten a glass of water from the sink before dinner and refused Sawyer's offers of beer and whiskey.

"Now we can get into the good stuff," Sawyer said, grinning. "You want to try some Russian whiskey, Luce?"

I shook my head. "This glass of wine was enough for me, but thanks. I'm going to clean up."

Sawyer had been more like himself today than I'd seen him in a long time. He'd taken a shower after going to the store and gone through his ginormous stack of mail. He and Kon and I had talked and laughed over dinner. I hated that he planned to drown his sorrows in alcohol again.

"No, not for me," Kon said as I carried my dessert plate over to the sink.

My brother balked. "Since when do you say no to whiskey?"

"I have practice in the morning. And you should, too."

I held my breath as I stood in front of the sink, not daring to look at them. Kon was taking a more direct approach than me, and while I wasn't sorry about it, I also wasn't sure how Sawyer would take it.

"I'm not on the team anymore," he said dismissively.

"You should be," Kon said. "We need you."

"Pfft. You guys have plenty of young bucks."

Kon came over to the sink, where he put his dishes on the counter.

"We need experience," he said, turning to face Sawyer.

I couldn't help turning, too, so I could try to read the emotions on my brother's face. He was looking down at the table, lost in his own thoughts. Kon and

I stayed still, both of us seeming to understand that Sawyer needed us not to talk right now, but to listen.

"I lost my reason," he finally said, gutting me. "It's no secret. Hockey's hard on your body and your mind, but I played for Annie. For our life together. For the kids we planned to have, so they could go to good colleges and we could..." He sighed and shrugged. "But it doesn't matter anymore."

It was all I could do not to break down in tears and run over to hug him. Kon remained in place, though, and I did, too. I couldn't cry and mourn with Sawyer forever; at some point, he had to find new reasons to get up in the morning and *live*.

"I do not have a family," Kon said. "Only my elderly grandmother back in Russia, and she refuses to take any more money from me." A small smile played on his lips, telling me he was very fond of her. "I play for...proud." He glanced at me, his brow furrowed. "Was that the right word?"

"Pride," I said softly. "But you were really close."

"Pride," he said, turning to look at Sawyer again. "I play because so many want to and never get to. Where I am from, playing a game for millions of dollars is a dream. I play so children in Russia know that they can play if they work hard."

Sawyer nodded. "I know, man, and I think you're a rock star. But I don't think I can go back."

I cleared my throat. "It might be nice to have something to focus your energy on, you know?"

"I've let myself go. I'd have to work my ass off to even have a chance at going back, but I don't think I'd be doing the team any favors. I'm not the player I used to be."

With that, he stood up and brought his plate over. "So that means more whiskey for me, I guess. You need help cleaning up, Luce?"

My heart sank. "No, I've got it."

He left the room, Kon staying behind and silently helping me clear the table.

"You don't have to help," I said.

"I know."

He started rinsing dishes and loading them into the dishwasher, methodically placing each piece of silverware onto the holder above the top rack. He put all the spoons in a row, then followed with the forks and then the knives.

"Do you get to see your grandma very often?" I asked as I hand-washed the stockpot I'd made the chicken and dumplings in.

"No. She refuses to leave Russia and I cannot go there."

"Why not?" I cringed as soon as the words were out. "I mean, if you don't mind me asking."

"I do not mind. Many athletes and actors won't

return to Russia for politics reasons."

The way he used the word *politics* instead of *political* brought a small smile to my lips. For such a serious guy, he was actually really cute. Not that I'd noticed.

"Makes sense," I said as I rinsed the pot. "People get detained for no reason."

"It is"

He was cut off by the shrill bleat of what sounded like an alarm, so loud it filled the room and echoed.

"Is that the fire alarm?" I asked him, my heart pounding.

Sawyer ran into the room, his expression intent.

"That's my security system," he said. "Kon, stay with Lucy. Do *not* let her out of your sight."

His security system. Nate. I knew he'd come looking for me, and since he knew I had information that could destroy him, I was terrified of what might happen.

"Sawyer, no," I said, following him up the stairs to his bedroom.

I ran to catch up with him, and by the time I got there, he was opening a wall safe in the master bedroom closet. Kon was right on my heels.

Sawyer pulled a handgun from the safe and loaded it. My knees weakened at what was unfolding in front of my eyes.

"Sawyer, no," I pleaded. "You don't know who you're messing with. We need to lock ourselves in a room and call the cops."

"The hell we do. If he came looking for trouble, he just found it."

"Who?" Kon asked, his gaze more intense than ever.

"Lucy's ex is after her," Sawyer said.

Kon nodded and reached out his hand. "Give me the gun. You stay with her."

"I know how to shoot," Sawyer protested.

"Just trust me," Kon said. "Give it to me and go to a room without windows."

Sawyer passed him the gun, taking another one from the safe and loading it. Jesus. He had an arsenal in there.

"Do not come out until I call and tell you it's safe," Kon said, checking something on the gun.

He left the room then, and I was on the edge of passing out. Shit was getting real, and I couldn't outrun it anymore.

CHAPTER SIX

Kon

A SURGE of adrenaline raced through me and my heart pounded against my chest. I hadn't felt a rush like this in a long time. Not since I'd left Russia. It was still familiar, though, and I mentally braced myself as I made my way down the stairs. The shrill echoes of the alarm kept me focused, my only purpose to keep my friends safe. I didn't know what the fuck Lucy's ex thought he was doing, if this was him, but I was going to find out. The thought of him coming after her made my blood boil. And frankly, despite his quick response tonight, Sawyer was generally in no shape to protect them if someone broke into the house.

The front door was still locked up tight, so I headed for the sliding glass doors that led out to the backyard.

Also still secured.

I glanced into the kitchen and dining room as I passed by, and both were empty. The living room was also just as we'd left it. I didn't think anyone had managed to get into the house, not with the alarm going off like a fucking bullhorn, but something had tripped the sensors.

Police sirens told me help was on the way and I decided to go back upstairs. Though I was here legally, I wasn't a US citizen, this wasn't my house, and the gun in my hand wasn't registered to me either. It was probably best not to greet the cops with a weapon, no matter what the situation was. I'd spent six weeks in a Russian jail once, and that was enough to keep me on the straight and narrow for the rest of my life, no matter where I lived.

"Anything?" Sawyer asked me, coming out of the guest bathroom and taking the gun I offered.

I shook my head. "Whoever it was didn't get in. Alarm probably scared them away."

"Fuck." He turned to Lucy, who'd come out behind him. "Why didn't you tell me he was crazy?"

Her eyes filled with tears. "I didn't—"

"Let's not talk about that now," I interjected

quickly, seeing how upset she was. "You have to deal with the police."

A loud banging on the front door announced their arrival.

Sawyer hurried down the hall toward the stairs and I took a moment to focus on Lucy. "You're okay?"

She nodded, swiping at her eyes. "I'm so sorry about all of this."

"This is not your fault." I reached out, closing my hand on one side of her waist. "Everything is going to be okay."

She nodded, crossing her arms over her chest protectively.

Damn.

She was shaking.

I reached out and pulled her against me, wrapping my arms around her tightly. "Don't worry. Sawyer and I won't let anything happen to you."

She was stiff at first but then practically melted against my chest.

I gently stroked her back, wishing I could say or do something to make her feel better. *Safer.* I wanted to offer to stay here, to help keep an eye on things, but I knew Sawyer wouldn't go for that.

We stood there for a minute or so and I closed my eyes. I liked the way she felt in my arms. Soft and sweet and feminine. So goddamn feminine. And she smelled good. Like cinnamon and apples.

Like something I wanted to lick.

Shit.

What the fuck was I thinking?

Luckily, she chose that moment to pull away, slowly running her hands down her face.

"I, um, thank you." She shifted from one foot to the other. "I think I'm okay now. It was just jarring. The alarm and…everything."

"I know." Our eyes locked and the jolt of lightning between us made my body tingle with need.

Then it was gone, almost as if I'd imagined it.

"We should, uh, probably go talk to the police." She nodded toward the voices now coming from downstairs.

"Maybe you need restraining order?"

"Yeah. I don't know. Maybe." She walked toward the staircase and I followed.

Talking to the police was my least favorite thing under any circumstances, but I had to remind myself this wasn't Russia and I hadn't done anything wrong. Sawyer seemed to have everything under control, talking animatedly to two officers as Lucy and I walked into the room. They turned, immediately firing questions in her direction.

She seemed exhausted, and once again the need

to protect her was overwhelming. I stood behind her, one hand at the small of her back, hoping to let her know I was there for her.

"Holy shit." The younger of the two policemen stared at me intently, his eyes suddenly widening. "You're Konstantin Volkov. And Sawyer Cain!" He smacked himself in the forehead. "It took me a minute to figure out why you looked familiar. I'm a huge Mavericks fan!" His face lit up with a smile, as if forgetting all about why he was here.

"Yes. Thank you." I spoke quietly, giving him a pointed look that I hoped would remind him of the situation at hand.

A slight flush crept up his neck and he cleared his throat. "Anyway, it looks like someone tried to open the window of a back room." He pointed toward what Sawyer and Annie called the den. "The security people told the dispatcher where the alarm was tripped. It was one of the rear windows and we found damage to the windowsill and broken shrubbery there."

"We can call a forensics unit to get fingerprints," the other policeman said, looking from Sawyer to Lucy. They eyed me with interest, but I didn't say or do anything, and they made notes as Lucy told them about Nate.

"Have you thought about a restraining order?" the younger cop asked.

"You think a restraining order is going to keep him from trying again?" Sawyer demanded, hands on his hips.

"We don't know for sure it was Nate," Lucy whispered.

"Bullshit." Sawyer looked pissed. And the most lucid he'd been in months.

I didn't know if this was good or bad.

"We can assign a few officers to patrol the street," the older cop said. "But I don't know for how long."

"Yeah, let's do that. Anything is better than nothing." Sawyer started talking about updating his security system, something I didn't know much about, so I kept my hand at Lucy's back.

The only thing I could do short term was offer her my support.

Long term, I needed to find her dickweed of an ex and kick his ass.

IT WAS a long night and I hated leaving but the police had left a patrolman out front for the rest of the night. I planned to stop by after practice today, just to make sure Lucy was okay, but my gut told me her ex wouldn't try again right away. No, he would watch and wait for the right time to make another move. That's what I would have done had I been in his shoes, and I didn't like this situation at all.

"Hey." Wes stopped me the moment I got to the arena. "I heard there was an incident at Sawyer's last night, but he's not answering my texts. You know anything about it?"

I nodded. "I was there. I don't know the whole story, but Lucy recently broke up with her boyfriend and they think it was him, trying to break into the house."

"For what?" Wes asked in confusion. "Does he have a history of abuse?"

I shrugged. "I don't know. She does not talk about him so much, and last night did not seem the time to ask many questions."

"I need to get over there," he said, running a hand through his hair. "I'm just so fucking busy. And, don't say anything to anyone yet, but we just found out Hadley's pregnant and she's been super sick so I'm trying to pick up the slack with the kids when I'm home."

When our previous team captain and his wife had died, Wes and his now-wife Hadley had taken custody of their two children, so they had their hands full.

"Congratulations," I said. "But don't worry. I'll be there every day we're not on the road. Even if it's just to stop by and say hello."

"Yeah, but it shouldn't all be on you. The team needs to step up. Even if this wasn't happening to Lucy, we should be trying harder with Sawyer."

"He said he may not be coming back," I said slowly. "That he has nothing to play for anymore."

"Jesus fucking Christ." Wes shook his head. "We need him. I need to make the time to see him. We obviously need to talk."

"I told him the same, but he is in a dark place." I tapped the side of my head with one finger. "Annie's death has changed him."

"Everything okay with Sawyer?" Nash joined us, frowning slightly.

I repeated the story for him and he growled. "What the fuck? Who is this guy? Do we need to go find him?"

"Believe me, I want to," I said. "I just don't know where to look."

"All right, settle down. Let's let the police do their jobs," Wes said sternly, eyeing us. "We don't need anyone winding up in jail."

I grimaced.

Definitely not.

But I'd risk it if it meant keeping people I cared about safe.

We headed into the dressing room where a group of guys were already locking up their things and changing.

"I bought a ring!" Boone called out when he saw us.

I managed not to roll my eyes. I didn't like Boone's girlfriend. Not that I'd ever tell him that, but something about her rubbed me the wrong way. As far as I could tell, none of the wives or girlfriends I knew spent time with her and she didn't come to many team events. Boone's excuse was always that she was shy or tired or something else. I thought he deserved better, but that wasn't the kind of thing you told your buddies.

"Congratulations!" Wes said, shaking his hand.

"Good luck with that." Nash told him, laughing.

"When are you gonna propose to Sariah?" Boone countered, referring to Nash's girlfriend.

"We *just* moved in together," Nash protested. "Give it a minute, would you?"

"Stay the hell away from me," Rory said, shuddering. "It's like this monogamy bullshit is contagious. One minute, half the team was single. Now you're all dropping like flies."

"You just say that because no one wants your

scraggly, *Duck Dynasty*-looking ass," Boone told him. Rory had been growing a beard since before the playoffs and now it was long and bushy, reaching his chest.

"The ladies *beg* to ride this baby," Rory said, wiggling his eyebrows as he stroked his hand down his beard. "Nothing like having a beard full of pussy—"

"You are disgusting," Lars said, making a face at him.

"Like Sheridan doesn't ride your—"

"Do not finish that sentence!" Lars glared, pointing a finger at him.

Rory just laughed. "You're all just jealous because the ladies love me." He playfully wiggled his hips.

"You're seriously delusional," Nash said, shaking with laughter.

"Hey, Kon, you wanna go out tonight?" Rory called to me, still moving his hips back and forth suggestively. "Find some honeys to spend a little *quality time* with."

"Sorry. Not tonight. I have plans."

"Aw, you suck."

"Date?" Boone asked quietly, cocking a brow.

"Helping Sawyer with something," I replied.

Helping him make sure Lucy was safe qualified, right?

"I can't do anything tonight. Missy and I have plans, but I'll head over there soon," he said. "I've missed his cranky ass."

"He is even worse now. You won't recognize him."

"Great. Looking forward to it."

I couldn't tell if he was being sarcastic or not, but either way, it would be good for the guys to spend time with Sawyer. Even if they couldn't get through to him, nothing would happen to Lucy while any of us were there. It was just a matter of making that happen as often as possible while simultaneously figuring out how the hell to keep them both safe when we were on the road.

CHAPTER SEVEN

Lucy

THE LIGHT SNOW coating the ground crunched under my boots as I approached Morelli Brothers, the little bakery I'd read rave reviews about online. It was only mid-November, but snow always made me feel like Christmas was near.

I couldn't go there yet, thoughfirst I had to figure out what to do for Thanksgiving. Sawyer and I had been invited to his teammate Wes and his wife Hadley's home for the holiday next week, but Sawyer refused to go. Our mom couldn't get away from caring for her sister, so I either had to convince Sawyer that we should celebrate with his team or cook a meal for the two of us myself.

And while I loved cooking, the thought of spending yet another day cooped up in Sawyer's house watching him drink beer and feel sorry for himself wasn't appealing.

I'd snuck out this morning while he was asleep on the couch. Not only did I need some fresh air, I wasn't going to live in fear of Nate. It had been several days since someone had set off Sawyer's security system, and I was ready to move on.

Just as I was about to walk into the bakery, my phone buzzed in my coat pocket with a text.

Kon: I would love to, thanks. What should I bring?

I smiled at the message on my screen. I'd texted him just before leaving Sawyer's house to invite him over again for dinner tonight.

Something inside me had shifted the night he'd gone looking for our potential home intruder with a gun. Kon had made me feel cared for and protected. Safe. The intensity I always saw in his gaze was mixed with confidence. He knew he was capable, and I sensed he also knew he was sexy as hell.

Not that I'd noticed. But when he held me the other night, I'd felt how rock hard his body was. It was like being hugged by a brick wall. And I didn't hate it.

I texted him back.

Lucy: Don't bring anything. Just be there by 6.

Kon: See you then.

Ugh, that awkward moment when you don't know whether to send another text or not. I decided to go with a reaction to his text instead. That created a new dilemma, though. Thumbs-up or heart emoji?

What the hell. I went with the heart. I did love that he was coming over tonight, because it meant I'd have someone other than my brother to talk to for a change. I also loved cooking for people. And if I accidentally ran into him and got another brick wall hug, that would be a bonus.

Nate and I had only been together for around nine months, and we hadn't touched each other in the past two months. Even before things got tense, he was never the type to comfort me with a hug or a kind word. Hell, he'd never even given me an orgasm in bed, which he said was my fault because I had "an unusually small clit." The red flags had been waving wildly, but had I noticed them? Nope.

As soon as I opened the door to Morelli Brothers, the scent of freshly baked bread made me smile and pause for a second.

The bakery was a huge, open space. I could see people working in the back, pushing loaves of bread and sheet pans of cookies into huge ovens, or pulling them out and adding them to one of the tall cooling racks on wheels.

The walls were decorated with vintage St. Louis news stories and ads. I stepped closer to one, which was a framed photo and magazine story about the Morelli Brothers, who were standing side by side and grinning at the camera.

"I'm the handsome one," a man behind the counter boomed. "Luigi."

His hair was peppered with gray now, and his belly was more pronounced, but I recognized his smile from the photo.

Looking back at the photo, I squinted at its caption. "Luigi and Mario Morelli? Really?"

"Really," he said, sounding weary of explaining it. "We're fifty-three and fifty-six—born before those cartoon guys made our names famous."

"That's pretty neat," I said, walking up to the glass display case at the front counter. "So what's your specialty?"

"Our specialty?" He shrugged, smile still in place. "Anything baked at Morelli Brothers will make you wonder whether you may have passed away unexpectedly and you're now in heaven. Our bread will make you weep with the knowledge that you've ever eaten any other kind."

I laughed. "That's quite an endorsement."

"What would you like a sample of? Tasting is believing."

"Hmm…" I scanned the baked goods, my gaze landing on a brownie drizzled with caramel and covered with chopped pecans. "Wow. Everything looks so good, but that brownie is calling my name."

Luigi nodded and reached into the case, cutting a generous piece off of a brownie in the very back. He placed it on a little napkin and passed it to me.

It was just after nine in the morning, a little early for a brownie, but what the hell? I bit into it and moaned with satisfaction.

"Did I lie to you?" Luigi asked.

I shook my head, covering my mouth with a hand as I chewed. "It's amazing. That caramel."

"Mario makes our caramel fresh every morning. Best in the world."

"Wow. I thought I made good brownies, but that one puts me to shame."

Luigi put his arms up in a *what can I say* motion. "Let us make your brownies from now on."

I resisted the urge to pop the rest of the brownie into my mouth immediately. "I'll definitely be buying some of those."

He gave me a stern look. "You gonna try and pass them off as yours?"

I laughed, and he grinned in response.

"If I thought I could get away with it, I totally would," I admitted. "But I'm making dinner for my brother and one of his friends, and if they ask me to make them again…"

"You just come right back to Morelli Brothers," he said. "We're open six days a week."

"Noted." I scanned the case again. "I was kind of hoping for something that I could use to make Italian beef sandwiches."

"You can't go wrong with our French bread," he said.

"Crusty rolls!" a male voice called out.

Luigi waved the voice off. "Don't listen to him."

A head popped up from beneath the counter. I recognized him from the photo—it was Mario, a thinner, balder version of Luigi, and he seemed to be repairing something.

"Are you using au jus?" Mario asked.

One of his dark, bushy eyebrows was covered in flour, making it white. I smiled and nodded.

"What's an Italian beef without au jus?" I asked.

He yelled out his approval, pumping his fist. "She knows her Italian beef! And trust me, you need a good sturdy bread to soak up all that juice."

"You just made the case for French bread!" Luigi cried, throwing his arms in the air. "Juice rolls right off a crusty roll."

Mario stood, meeting his brother's gaze. "Did

you just get off the boat from Italy? You have to let it soak."

"It could soak for eighteen years and it still wouldn't taste as good as my French bread."

Mario gave him a disgusted look, waving him off. "This is why Nonna gave me her hot cross bun recipe."

Luigi lowered his brows, pointing at his brother's chest. "You got that recipe for one reason and one reason alone. You're a butt-kisser and everyone knows it."

A woman who looked about my age approached the counter, rolling her eyes and smiling slightly. "Don't mind these two. We have some great hoagies that just came out of the oven. I think you'd be really happy with them for Italian beef sandwiches."

I gave her a grateful look, because I didn't want to choose between the recommendations of the two owners.

"Yeah, don't mind us," Mario said, putting an arm around his brother's shoulders. "We're just passionate about our baking."

"I understand."

"What else can we get you?" Luigi asked, the argument already forgotten.

"I'll take six of those brownies and ten hoagie rolls."

A line had formed behind me, so the woman asked the next customer for their order and Luigi sent another employee to get my hoagie rolls.

"So, this friend of your brother," he said as he put my brownies into a plastic container. "Is he someone you're trying to impress?"

My cheeks warmed as I considered his question. I mean…I wasn't *not* trying to impress him, but it felt weird to admit it out loud. Especially when I'd just ended a relationship. I was here to get Sawyer back on his feet and then I was relocating to a new place for a fresh start. Not just because I wanted to, but because I *had* to.

"I always try to impress with my cooking," I said, winking at Luigi.

"What's your name?"

"Lucy."

He looked at me over the rim of his glasses. "Lucy, any guy who gets to eat your homemade Italian beef needs to work hard for you, understand?"

He reminded me of my grandpa, and I felt a sudden pang of sadness. I missed him. "I do."

"Good." He closed the plastic container. "You make him wine and dine you, and if he makes one wrong move, send him packing."

I nodded. "I'll remember that."

He grabbed the container of hoagie rolls from the employee who had gotten them from the back, then put both containers into a paper bag. When he passed it to me, I asked, "How much do I owe you?"

He shook his head. "No charge for first-timers. You just come back and tell us how dinner goes, okay, Lucy?"

I pushed my wallet back into my purse, touched by his generosity and kindness. "I definitely will. Thanks, Luigi."

It was snowing harder when I walked out the door, but I didn't feel the cold. There were still good people in this world. Wherever I ended up, though I wouldn't know a soul, I hoped I met people as nice as Luigi Morelli.

CHAPTER EIGHT

Kon

I was distracted when I got to practice, thinking about seeing Lucy again tonight. Something had shifted between us that night at her house, and I knew she felt it too or she wouldn't have invited me back. I didn't know what to do about it since I wasn't interested in anything beyond sex and she was leaving town anyway, but the pull was too strong to ignore. There was something there, and the way her body had fit against mine made me remember what it was like to have a woman in my life.

I'd never been one of those guys who got distracted by women. Back in Russia, my life had been rough so I ran with an even tougher crowd.

Both male and female. Some of the girls in my inner circle had been prostitutes because spreading their legs was the only way they could earn enough money to eat. It wasn't like it was here in the US, where you could get a job at McDonald's and sleep on your friend's couch. Where I came from, there were no McDonald's and barely enough couches for the people who lived there, much less anyone else.

There was no shame in admitting I'd slept with those girls. We'd all needed kindness in our lives, and sometimes that was the only way to get it. There had been no money in those exchanges. It had been about survival. And finding tiny moments of pleasure wherever and however you could get it. We'd understood each other. Been there for each other. Helped each other. Eventually, one of those women had saved me.

Svetlana.

Sweet, beautiful, and horribly abused, she'd risked everything to save my life one night. Then it had been up to me to take care of her. And I had. I'd made her my girlfriend and eventually brought her to America with me. We'd had a good life even if we hadn't been in love the way we should have been. In retrospect, I understood how unhealthy our relationship had been. Instead of a bond that grew from love and respect, ours had been forged from mutual history, need, and pain. We'd understood that we were probably too broken to love anyone but each other and had settled into what I'd thought was something good. The money I made and the life we'd been building here in the US would give us a strong, comfortable future.

Something neither of us had ever dared to imagine for ourselves.

That she would throw it away for a prick like Keegan Miller was beyond me.

Even now that she was long gone, I couldn't understand why she'd picked *him*. If she'd fallen for almost any other of my teammates, I would've been hurt but it would make sense. Nash and Boone and most of the others were stellar human beings who would have made her happy, probably taken even better care of her than I had. Except, of course, those guys would never have fooled around with a teammate's girlfriend.

Irony at its finest.

I'd been so lost in thought I hadn't been paying attention to what was going on around me and as I got to my locker to change, I spotted Boone sitting on a bench, not moving. He looked…upset? I wasn't sure, because aside from something serious like death, we didn't bring personal problems to practice. Ever. That was how we rolled in hockey, and it had been no different in Russia or the other team I'd played for here in North America.

I walked over and kicked his shoe. "What is wrong with you?"

He didn't move. I was about to give him a playful shove when he whispered, "She said no."

His voice was so quiet, it took a second for his words to register. "What?"

He motioned with his hand, as if shooing me away. "Just let me brood. I'll be fine in a minute."

I wanted to say something, but I wasn't sure what. "You dodged a bullet" didn't seem prudent so I merely nodded and walked to my locker and opened it.

Nash caught my eye and gave me a questioning look. I didn't want to say anything, so I held up my left hand, pointed to my ring finger, and then made a slashing motion across my throat with my other hand. His eyebrows rose in surprise, and he glanced at Boone. He seemed to respect Boone's need for silence, though, and gave me a curt nod before beginning to undress.

More guys came in, chattering away, and Boone finally got up and started pulling off his street clothes.

Christ. I wasn't the touchy-feely type. That was Wes's job most of the time. But Wes didn't know what had happened and Boone was one of my best friends. I didn't do emotions, but I had to suck it up and at the very least do friendship. He'd been there for me when Svetlana had blown up my life.

"Hey." I waited until he was lacing up his skates. "You okay?"

"Nope. But I will be."

"What did she say?"

"She said I wasn't the kind of guy nice girls married." His voice got a little edgy, and I didn't blame him. "That I was a bad boy nice girls *fucked* until they found the men they were going to marry."

That was bullshit because while we all had moments of fuckery—sleeping with puck bunnies, talking trash, and living the lives of pro athletes—Boone was a good guy. One of the best. Smart, educated, and from a nice, middle-class family. His father came on the annual dads' trips wearing knee socks and sandals half the time, so incredibly proud of his son and so honored to hang with us, he didn't care how nerdy he was. His mom baked cookies whenever she was in town, feeding all of us and learning the names of each of our wives, girlfriends, and children. And there was a fucking ton of them.

I'd known Missy wasn't the woman for Boone but I'd never imagined she thought she was too good for him. Fuck her and her arrogance.

"I won't say anything bad about her," I said slowly, "because you two have broken up and gotten back together more than once, but you know she is full of shit, right? You are a good man and deserve better."

He didn't look at me, reaching for a roll of tape and absently fingering it.

"Did you and Missy break up again?" Rory demanded, overhearing the last part of what I'd said.

I winced, because I hadn't meant for anyone to hear, but what Missy had said to Boone pissed me off. I *really* disliked when people fucked with my friends.

Boone blew out a breath and looked up. Luckily, only a few players were still in here, the rest either out in the hallway or already on the ice.

"She said no," he said, loud enough for everyone in the general vicinity to hear. "And while I'm prepared for you all to bust my balls over it, I would appreciate it not being today. Give me a day or so and then give it your best shot."

Wes frowned. "Dude, we all have fucking PhDs in ballbusting. It's part of the job. But we don't kick our brothers when they're down."

"First we lift you up," Lars said quietly.

"Then we knock you back on your ass," Nash

added, a smile quirking on his lips. "Once you're ready for it."

"Thanks." Boone looked away. "Just getting it straight in my head." He got up and clomped out of the room on his skates, calling for one of the trainers.

We all looked at each other.

"I have plans tonight," I said after a moment. "But someone needs to take him out and get him drunk. He shouldn't be alone." I looked at Rory since he was single and always up for partying. "Can you handle this without being a dumbass?"

Rory flipped me the bird. "Hey, I may be an asshole seventy-five percent of the time, but I got him. Leave it to me."

———

I GOT to Sawyer's place just before six and grabbed the bottle of Napa Valley cabernet I'd picked up. Lucy liked Napa Valley wines, and though she'd told me not to bring anything, it felt weird not to. We hadn't had a pot to piss in but on the rare occasion we went somewhere, my grandmother found some-thing to bring. A bouquet of flowers picked from a field, a small dessert she'd put together, something. You didn't arrive empty-handed, and while I was a grown man now who didn't have to worry about impressing anyone with my manners, I still wanted her to be proud of me.

"Hi." Lucy opened the door just as I lifted my hand to knock.

"Hello." I leaned over and brushed my lips across her cheek. She smelled delicious again, making it hard to remember why I was there. "Uh, this is for you. I hope you like it."

"I told you not to bring anything." Her eyes met mine with a curious smile, as if she'd noticed my bumble and knew she'd been the cause.

"My grandmother taught me it is impolite to arrive with nothing."

"My mother taught me the same," she said. "But this is different."

"It's not." I followed her into the house, noting Sawyer was nowhere to be found. "Where is Sawyer?"

She made a face. "Showering."

"Is he no better?"

She sighed, shrugging one shoulder. "I thought for a minute, after that attempted break-in, he was, but now he's basically back to drinking all day. I'm running out of ideas, Kon." We walked into the kitchen where she checked something in the oven. "Oh, the bread is ready." She lifted a baking sheet of some kind, setting it on the counter. She'd just put it down when she let out a shriek, yanking her hand back and sticking her finger in her mouth.

"What happened?" I asked, hurrying over to her.

"It's stupid." She shook her head. "I accidentally hit the edge of the pan with my finger. I'm fine."

"Let me see." I held out my hand.

She opened her mouth, as if to protest, but then slowly held out her finger.

I grasped her hand and turned it over, gently running one of my fingers over the reddest area of hers. Her hand looked tiny compared to mine, but I liked touching her. Liked being this close to her.

"Does it hurt?" I asked after a moment.

"A little. I'll, uh, run cold water over it."

"*Da*. That is…good." I'd said *yes* in Russian because my English momentarily failed me as we stood there, her hand in mine, our eyes linked. She looked so pretty, her plump lower lip between her teeth and her golden hair bouncing around her shoulders.

I couldn't remember the last time I'd wanted to kiss someone so much.

"What the hell are you doing?" Sawyer's loud voice made us jump, but I turned, giving him a dirty look.

"She burned her hand. Can you grab some ice?"

"Oh." He stared for a moment before moving toward the refrigerator. "I think there's some lavender oil upstairs. Annie swore by it for burns."

Lucy and I seemed to hold our breaths as Sawyer got a big ball of craft ice out of the freezer. This was the first time he'd mentioned Annie in passing with no hesitation or reaction of any kind.

"Here." He handed Lucy the ice ball. "Let me run upstairs and grab it."

We watched him go and our eyes met. "Did he just…talk about Annie?" she whispered.

"He did." I grabbed a paper towel and handed it to her. "Use this for the ice or it will be too cold."

"Thank you."

It felt like something momentous had just happened, but we didn't have time to say anything more about it because Sawyer was back with the lavender oil and Lucy took it from him. While she tended to her finger, Sawyer started putting the warm rolls she'd just pulled from the oven into a basket she'd prepared.

"I hear Boone's girlfriend dumped him again," Sawyer said.

"You heard?" I asked in surprise.

"Rory texted, asked if I wanted to go out and help him get Boone drunk." Sawyer shrugged. "Not really interested in going anywhere since I have plenty of booze at home, but I feel for the guy. Getting dumped during a proposal is shitty."

"It would be good for you to be there for your friend the way he's been there for you," Lucy said, glancing over her shoulder.

"Don't start, Luce." He rolled his eyes at her.

"She is right," I said, leaning against the counter and watching him.

"Not you too. Jesus, can you guys give me a fucking break?" He stomped out of the room and Lucy sighed.

"Like I said, one step forward and two steps back."

CHAPTER NINE

Lucy

"I HAD A FEELING THIS MIGHT HAPPEN," I told Kon as I walked back into the family room from the basement. "He's out cold."

Kon shrugged. "Probably for the best. He did not get in as much beer as usual and he can sleep off his mood."

Sawyer had gotten salty—again—when I suggested he lay off the alcohol. He drank unconsciously, just cracking open can after can. It was hard for me to watch him trying to drown his feelings in alcohol, but he balked when I tried to get him to stop. He'd gone down to his man cave in the basement nearly an hour ago and when I'd gone to check on him just now, I'd found him passed out on a leather sofa in the room with all his hockey memorabilia.

"Would you like another glass?" Kon asked, getting up from the couch and walking toward my empty wineglass on the coffee table.

"I will later, but for now, will you help me with something?"

"Of course." He arched his brows and grinned. "What is that smile for?"

"I want to do something that may not amuse my brother but will definitely amuse me."

Kon laughed, a rare sound from him. "Nothing amuses Sawyer anymore."

"This might get a laugh out of him. You know how there used to be pictures of him and Annie on that wall?"

Kon turned and looked at the light gray wall behind the biggest couch in the room and nodded.

"I assume he took them all down because it was too hard to look at them," I said. "I was hoping you could text your teammates for some funny selfies and I thought we'd decorate the wall with those instead. I went to Target earlier and bought a bunch of frames."

We stood close enough that I could see the flecks of brown swirling in his hazel eyes, and as a couple seconds of silence passed, I wanted to ditch my picture idea and just stay lost in those eyes.

"That is a nice idea," he finally said. "I will text the team."

I took a deep breath in and slowly let it out, my heart slowing to its usual speed again. There was something about being alone with Kon that I liked. A lot.

He'd brushed past me in the kitchen earlier when we were cleaning up after dinner and my pulse had pounded then, too. An attraction to him was the last thing I needed right now, but I couldn't deny I felt it.

"I'll go get the frames," I said. "When you get the pictures, we can print them at the drugstore that's not far from here."

By the time I got back downstairs with the bags of frames, he'd already gotten several selfies. Wes had sent one of him and his kids and Rory had sent one of him and Boone cheering at a bar.

I was peeking over his shoulder when Kon pulled up the one Nash had sent. I gasped when I saw an up-close dick pic.

"Fucking bastard," Kon muttered. "I'm sorry."

He quickly texted Nash a response, his brow furrowed. When he read the response, he shook his head.

"He said it was an accident. I don't believe him."

I laughed as I unpacked a frame. "How do you *accidentally* take a photo of your dick and balls and send it to someone?"

Kon was furiously sending another message. "He said that one was meant for his girlfriend."

"Tell him we're putting it up on Sawyer's wall."

"He would like that. Nash…has very high self-esteem." He shook his head again. "Sorry about that."

I waved it off. "Trust me, it's not the first time I've gotten a dick pic. And I've never wanted to see one. Why do men do that? You're having a perfectly nice text conversation and then suddenly they send a photo of their penis. I don't get it."

"They think it will impress women."

"I suppose, but a picture of them folding laundry would be better. Any guy can play with himself, but a man who takes care of business is sexy."

Kon gave me an amused look. "I am great at laundry."

"Really? Tell me more."

Putting his phone in his jeans pocket, he walked over to me. "First, I sort into whites, colors, and towels."

I fanned myself. "Okay, that's hot."

He nodded. "I use Tide laundry detergent and an unscented fabric softener."

I furrowed my brow. "Wait a minute. You actually do your own laundry?"

That surprised me, because Sawyer had his laundry picked up by a laundry service and it was returned washed and folded.

"Of course," Kon said. "And I fold it as soon as the dryer buzzes."

I feigned a moan. "You're getting me all worked up here."

He was so close now I could touch him, but I had a partially wrapped picture frame in my hands. That was probably for the best, because even though I *could* touch him, I knew I shouldn't.

"I hang up everything I can," he said, his tone lower and softer now. "And I even fold my T-shirts and stack them on a shelf in my closet."

I swallowed hard, my mind no longer on laundry. "You're officially sexy."

"So are you. But I knew that the minute I saw you."

He sank his teeth into his lower lip, our gazes locked, my heart pounding. I had no place to put the picture frame, so I lowered my hand and held it next to my leg.

Kon leaned in and I tipped my face up slightly. He was right on the edge of kissing me when his phone started blaring...*The A-Team* theme song?

It was so loud I jumped, ruining the moment. Kon cringed.

"I am sorry. That is…" He took out his phone and looked at the screen. "It's Lars. That is a joke between the team because he recently discovered *The A-Team* and he thinks it is the best show ever made."

I busted out laughing. "*The A-Team!*"

Kon shook his head. "You do not want to see his Mr. T impersonation."

"Go ahead and answer it," I said. "It could be important."

He gave me a wary look. "Not as important as this."

My crush on him doubled in size as I smiled. "I'm not going anywhere. Just see what he wants."

He answered the call, which gave me a chance to put down the damn picture frame. Now I'd have both hands free to roam over Kon's body when he kissed me.

"No, you can't," he said to Lars. "He is already passed out…no, Lucy and I are using those to hang up on his wall and it will ruin the surprise…just send the fucking selfie."

He rolled his eyes and looked at me, shaking his head. "Just the picture…no. *No*…I don't know. I sent it out on the text thread the whole team is on…no… Lars…fuck."

He ended the call and met my gaze. "They are coming over to help."

"Who?"

"Lars is going to invite the entire team over here."

"Over *here*?" My jaw dropped. "You mean now?"

He nodded as I looked around Sawyer's family room. "But this place needs cleaning, and I don't have snacks. And if he wakes up to a houseful of people, Sawyer's going to flip his shit."

"Sawyer knows how the guys are. Lars is…he helps by doing things. They feel bad that they haven't checked in on him more. And they don't care what the house looks like, Lucy."

I blew out a breath. "Okay, well…we'll just roll with it, I guess."

He put his phone back in his jeans pocket and walked over to me, his gaze intense. "We will not be alone for long, so I am not missing this."

Putting his hand on the side of my throat, he gently brushed his thumb over my jawline. I inhaled sharply, something about his hand on my throat giving me butterflies. No man had ever done that, and it felt sensual and possessive.

He put his other hand on my hip, sliding it around

to my lower back as his lips met mine. We moved at the same time, pressing our bodies together as he deepened the kiss. His fingers cupped the back of my neck and he wrapped his entire arm around my waist, holding me tightly as he devoured my mouth with his.

I brought my arms around his neck, lost in the sensation of our kiss. Kon was outwardly stoic, but he kissed me with more passion than I'd ever felt before. He held me so tightly that I felt his erection pressing against my belly, and it only fueled my desire more.

When I finally had to pull away from him, breathless, he still held me close, running the tip of his nose along the side of mine.

"Sawyer will kill me for this," he whispered. "But I don't care."

I ran my fingers over the short, dark stubble on his cheek as he rested his forehead against mine. "I didn't know a kiss could be like that."

He gave me a soft, gentle kiss, relaxing his hold on me. "I have to stop now, or I won't be able to."

The butterflies were back. I wanted to know what that felt like—to make this man so crazy with lust that he couldn't hold back. I wanted it more than anything.

Kon didn't kiss me again, but he also didn't let me go. We just stood there holding on to each other. I rested my cheek on his shoulder and took in his clean, masculine scent.

It felt like time had stopped, but then it returned with the ring of the doorbell a few minutes later. Kon groaned and I unhooked my arms from his neck.

"Bastards," he muttered. "I will beat them with my stick at our next practice."

"They mean well," I reminded him. "I'll go answer it."

"No, let me. You should not answer the door."

Because of the attempted break-in the other night. I'd completely forgotten about it when I was wrapped in Kon's protective embrace.

"Oh, yeah. You're right."

Within twenty minutes, the house was filled with tall, boisterous hockey players. Lars had brought his wife Sheridan, who was warm and beautiful. Some of the guys had picked up the printed photos, Sheridan and I framed them, and Kon and Nash hung them.

As she pulled the next photo from the envelope, Sheridan screeched and then burst into laughter.

"What?"

She turned the photo around and I saw Nash's dick—again. I burst out laughing, too.

"The kid working the photo counter said he

wasn't supposed to develop it, but I slipped him a fifty," Rory said. "Figured this was something Sawyer needs to see every morning when he wakes up."

"Really?" Lars said to Nash with a glare.

Nash put his hands up in mock surrender. "Hey, I accidentally sent it. I never meant for this to happen."

"Accidentally." Sheridan lifted her fingers in an air quotes motion and gave me a look. "That's what they all say."

The photo of Nash's dick and balls was hung near the center of the wall, between a selfie of me and Kon and another of Rory sitting on the toilet giving a peace sign.

"So tasteful," I said, cracking up again.

"I can't believe he hasn't woken up from all this noise," Sheridan says.

"Once he's out, he's out," I said.

"Well, he's in for a surprise tomorrow."

Everyone finished their drinks and started heading out. Kon was the last one in the house, and he reluctantly looked at his watch and then at me.

"If I didn't have an early practice…"

"Another night," I said. "If you want."

"Oh, I want." He kissed me gently. "You will see how much I want, Lucy."

"See you soon?"

"As soon as I can." He kissed me again. "Arm the security system and text me if you need anything, okay?"

I nodded. "Good night."

He took a couple steps out the door, then turned and came back, kissing me again.

"Good night."

CHAPTER TEN

Kon

DESPITE WANTING to see Lucy again, duty called the following night. Boone had been struggling since his breakup with Missy and I could only handle one grief-stricken friend at a time. Sawyer was being incredibly difficult. He'd been a grumpy ass the last seven months. He needed to join the land of the living again, and I was willing to—gently—beat some sense into him if it came to that. However, tonight I was going to use his situation to snap Boone out of the funk he was in.

We met up at a sports bar in the suburbs, a place where we hung out when it was just a few of us. We couldn't come to places like this as a group because we were too recognizable, but when it was just two or three of us, it was a nice place to watch *Monday Night Football* or a basketball game. Personally, I thought American football was boring, but my teammates seemed to love it so I tried to follow as best I could.

"Do you want to talk about it?" I asked when the second quarter of the game ended and halftime started.

"About Missy?" He shook his head. "Not really. It was…eye opening. I had no idea she was using me. I just don't know for what since she obviously wasn't after my money. Like, am I really some kind of bad boy?" He wrinkled his nose as he turned to me. "I'll cop to being badass in bed, but the rest of it? And anyway, how come a guy who makes a lot of money, knows how to get a woman off, and doesn't abuse you isn't husband material? What the fuck is that about?"

"I do not understand either," I admitted. "You are very…" I paused, trying to think of the right phrase. "Normal? I don't know what word to use. I look like the bad boys you see on TV, maybe a biker or something. But you? You are very boring. Very much like someone's *husband*."

We both laughed since he understood what I was trying to say.

"And that's just it—she was kind of boring too. I thought a girl like that, someone sweet and kind of modest and very professional would be the right kind of woman to marry. Instead, she was using me to add a notch to her fucking bedpost. Fuck that and fuck her." He motioned to the bartender. "Bring us a couple of shots."

"Not for me," I said. "Someone has to drive."

"Oh, come on, live a little. We can Uber home if we have to."

Then I wouldn't have my truck in the morning. I could call someone to pick me up, but that was a hassle. I was only twenty-seven, but a little set in my ways and I hated not having my own vehicle. Having a way to escape if I needed to. My past stuck with me in some ways, no matter how much my life had changed.

But my buddy needed me.

So I'd do one shot and then we could order food. I'd be okay if I ate and drank plenty of water.

My phone buzzed in my pocket and I pulled it out, surprised to see Lucy's name flashing on the screen. We'd texted earlier, and I'd told her I would be going out with Boone tonight.

"Hi," I said. "You are okay?"

"No." She sounded breathless. "Today while I was out, I thought I saw this red SUV following me but it was hard to be sure and then it disappeared, so I forgot about it. But I was about to take the garbage cans out to the curb for pickup tomorrow and the same red SUV is parked across the street. I'm sure of it."

"Where is Sawyer?" I demanded.

She hesitated. "He's passed out in the basement. I tried to wake him up but he's out cold. Today is Annie's birthday, so he was worse than usual."

"What happened to the police security?"

"They were here for two nights and then that was the end of it."

Fuck.

"The alarm is set?"

"Yes. Once I saw that SUV, I immediately closed the garage door and double-checked that everything is locked."

"I am coming. Stay in the house, okay?"

"I will."

"Fifteen minutes." I threw a couple of twenties on the bar and turned to Boone. "I am sorry. I have to go."

"Was that Lucy? What's going on?" He stood up, frowning.

"We think her ex is stalking her but—" I cut myself off. "Long story. I don't have time."

"If something is going on, I'm coming too."

I hesitated but then nodded. It might be good to have backup and a witness since I had no idea what I might find.

Boone jumped into my truck instead of driving his own car and I drove to Sawyer's place faster than I should have. My chest was tight because I was both worried and annoyed. Lucy had been cagey about what had gone on with her ex. We never had much time alone together, to talk or anything else, but she needed to tell me the whole story if I was going to help. One way or another, I needed to know what was going on.

I saw the red SUV as soon as I turned the corner, and I pulled to a stop in front of Sawyer's town house. I turned off my truck, drumming my fingers on the steering wheel as I took in my surroundings and tried to decide how to approach this. The street was quiet, most people in for the night in this upscale suburban neighborhood.

"What are you going to do?" Boone asked me, following my gaze. I'd told him everything I knew on the drive over, so he seemed on edge as well.

"I want you to go in the house with Lucy," I said finally. "And be ready to call 9-1-1 if this guy tries anything."

"You sure?" He frowned. "I'm not a scary-ass

motherfucker like you, but I can hold my own in a fight."

I chuckled. "I have no doubt, but someone needs to be with Lucy. Just in case."

"Okay." He got out and jogged to the front door, ringing the bell.

I waited until she let him in before getting out of my truck. I needed to know why this guy was parked across from the house. If it turned out to be the guest of a neighbor, I'd apologize and move on. I didn't think so, though, and based on how scared Lucy had sounded, she didn't either.

I walked across the street and leaned down, knocking on the passenger side window.

The man in the driver's seat rolled the window down and glared at me. "What do you want?"

"I want to know why you're loitering on a private street." I leaned in, resting my forearms on the door and making sure he got a good look at the tattoos covering them. They weren't gang-affiliated or anything, but hopefully the Cyrillic letters spelling out my grandmother's name would give him Russian mob vibes or something equally intimidating.

"None of your fucking business."

I arched a brow and leaned in slightly. "My family lives on this street. There are children in some of these homes. The bus stop is over there." I motioned randomly with my head since I had no idea if there was a bus stop. "Trust me when I tell you they're going to notice a strange man parked on the street. Once the police are called, I'll be the least of your worries."

The man scowled. "I *am* the police. I'm here doing surveillance. That's all I can tell you."

"Do you have identification?"

"Excuse me?"

"ID. Do you have any? If you're a cop, let me see your badge."

"Listen, mister, I don't have to show you shit. Now how about you fuck off before I arrest your ass?" His growl turned nasty and I studied his face, making a mental note of his thick neck, curly dark hair, and bushy eyebrows. Impulsively, I pulled out my phone and snapped a picture of his face before he could stop me.

"What the—" He lunged toward me but I backed away from the car.

"If you were actually a policeman, you'd have ID." I made a show of typing on my phone. "But maybe the local police can verify—" I barely finished talking before he started the SUV and put it in gear. I took a step back as he took off down the street, taking a picture of his license plate as well.

As much as I wanted to handle this myself, we were probably going to have to call the police again.

I went to the door and Boone opened it. "What happened?"

"He left once I started questioning him."

"You have balls of steel, man."

"Where's Lucy?"

"She went to get a robe or something. Said she was cold."

I nodded. "And fucking Sawyer. He needs a… what do you call it? Come to Jesus?"

Boone nodded too. "Yeah. Lucy said he's out cold."

I heard her steps on the stairs and turned. As soon as she saw me, she ran across the room, throwing herself in my arms. I wrapped them around her tightly, holding her close even as I saw Boone giving me the side-eye and quirking up one of his eyebrows in question.

"Whoever it was is gone," I said quietly, ignoring Boone. "But I spoke to him. He was very suspicious. He said he was a policeman but left when I asked to see ID. I got a picture of his face and his license plate."

She sighed. "Damn it."

"You know who it is?" I showed her the picture.

"No, but Nate's brother is a detective in Spokane so he could've sent one of his buddies on the force."

"He would send someone across the country to find you? Why?"

"I don't...know."

She was lying, but I wasn't going to have this conversation with her in front of Boone. Anyway, right now I was more pissed at Sawyer. His constant drinking and lack of concern for Lucy, even on Annie's birthday, was unacceptable. This Nate fucker was a danger to Lucy. My gut rarely steered me wrong—it had kept me alive for years—and I trusted the feeling that something bad was going to happen if Lucy wasn't careful. And Sawyer needed to be awake and alert if it did.

"It's time for some tough love," I said after a moment. "Sawyer has to man the fuck up."

"Kon, I don't know if—" she began.

"You do things your way. Gentle and caring and soft. Boone and I are going to do things our way." Without a word, I turned and headed down the stairs to the basement, Boone on my heels.

As expected, Sawyer was passed out on the sectional there, a bottle of Jack Daniels in one hand, resting against his side, and a picture of Annie on his chest. God, I hated seeing him like this. But that was exactly why I was doing this. One way or another, he had to snap out of this state. See a therapist, go back-packing through South America, join the circus. I didn't know what he needed, but I knew for sure he would never forgive himself if something happened to Lucy.

"Hey. Wake up." I pulled the bottle and picture from his hands, setting them on the nearest table.

Sawyer grunted and turned over.

"Sawyer!" I raised my voice and gave his shoulder a shove. "Wake up!"

"Fuck…" He moaned sleepily, resting his arms over his face.

"Get up, Sawyer." I yanked him up by the shirt, pushing him into a sitting position. His head lolled to one side even as his eyes opened into slits of irritation.

"The fuck is wrong with you?" he rasped, his words slurred as he sneered.

"Do you have any idea what's going on around you while you drink yourself to death?" I snapped. I lightly slapped his cheeks. "Wake the fuck up and pay attention."

"Knock it off!" Sawyer swatted at me, tripping as he tried to get up and lunge at me. He landed on his stomach on the floor and while I hated being an asshole, this was what he needed. We'd tried every-thing else.

"Nate sent someone to watch your house!" I yelled. "To potentially try to break in again. To hurt Lucy. Do you hear what I'm telling you? Get up, Sawyer." I stood over him, hands on my hips. I glanced over at Boone who gave me a little nod, letting me know he agreed with what I was doing.

"Wh-what?" Sawyer was still face down on the floor but had lifted his head. "Lucy okay?"

"Yes, because she called *me* and I chased the guy off. What happens when I'm on the road? What happens when I'm at fucking practice? You can't fucking drink yourself into oblivion every goddamn night. I am very sorry Annie is gone, but Lucy is still here, and she needs you. Your sister needs you. What the fuck is wrong with you?"

There was a long silence as Sawyer tried to sit up. He was still completely wasted, barely able to keep his eyes open, and his movements were jerky and awkward. It was killing me not to help him, and the look on Boone's face told me he felt the same way, but Sawyer had to be the one to crawl out of his self-imposed hell. He had to care more about Lucy than the demons that were haunting him.

Finally, after three attempts to get back on the couch, I reached out a hand.

His bleary eyes met mine and neither of us moved. The ultimate standoff. He hated me for calling him on his bullshit and I hated doing it. But someone had to.

He finally slapped his palm against mine and let me haul him onto the couch.

"Where is she?" he asked, rubbing his eyes.

"Upstairs."

He nodded.

"I'm going to sleep here tonight," I said finally. "You need to sleep this off, but in the morning, you have to think about what you are doing. I cannot be here every night. And obviously Nate is not giving up."

Sawyer nodded wearily. "Fuck. I'm sorry."

"I am not the one you have to apologize to."

I turned and headed back up the stairs.

I'd made my point.

Now it was up to him.

CHAPTER ELEVEN

Lucy

"I CAN'T DO THIS." Sawyer put his head in his hands. "It's too much, Luce."

"You have to. I know it's hard"

"No, you don't!" he snapped. "You have no idea what this feels like. It feels like I'm dying, and this isn't how I want to go."

We were only around eighteen hours into Sawyer's detox and it was already hellish. He'd been asleep for more than half of it, Kon and Boone sleeping on recliners in the basement to make sure he didn't drink.

The three of us had poured out every drop of

alcohol we could find in the house, and there had been a lot. Kon had confiscated Sawyer's phone and wallet, and he wasn't giving them back until this was over. He was right—this was the tough love my brother needed.

"You were killing yourself with alcohol," I reminded him.

"So what? I get to make that choice."

"Not on my watch. And you wouldn't let me do it to myself, either."

He growled with frustration, scowling at me. "Everything was fine before you got here. This is all Nate's fault."

I pressed my lips together to hold in my sharp response. Everything hadn't been fine before I got here. Not with him, and sure as hell not with me. My life had turned into a living hell over the course of a month, and Sawyer didn't have a clue how scary it was.

"What's with the look on your face?" he demanded. "Kon's not here for you to look at when one of you thinks I'm being a jackass."

"Which is a lot," I said with a glare.

He got up from his seat on the couch, hands on his hips.

"I never asked any of you for help." He gestured

at the wall behind the couch. "Nash's dick is hanging on my goddamn wall and Kon's treating me like a prisoner in my own home."

I laughed bitterly. Kon and Boone were at practice, leaving me alone to deal with Sawyer's tirade. And we were just starting—it was going to get worse from here.

"Life is full of things we didn't ask for," I shot back. "What happened to Annie was brutally unfair. Did she ask for it?"

He flinched at the mention of her name.

"But still she was grateful," I said, tears welling in my eyes. "She never got angry at the world. And she wouldn't want you to, either."

Sawyer put his head in his hands. "What else is there, Luce? I drink to stop feeling like I want to burn the whole fucking world down."

The anguish in his tone was too much for me. Tears slid onto my cheeks as I walked over to him.

"We're going to find another way," I assured him. "Something besides hating the world and drinking to block it out."

He nodded, lowering his hands. "I need to do it slowly. Start by drinking less."

Kon had told me this would happen. That he would beg and rage and turn into a different person before this was over, but we had to stay the course. I knew he was right.

"The team doctor is coming over to evaluate you soon," I said. "He'll be monitoring you to make sure we're doing this the right way."

"I don't want fucking Morales in my fucking house treating me like some pathetic addict! I'm not even on the team anymore."

"Kon texted me that they were on their way about half an hour ago. They should be" A knock sounded on the front door. "That's probably them."

"Fuck," he muttered as I left to answer the door.

Tough love. Tough love. Tough love.

I could do this.

When I opened the door, Kon, Boone, another Mavericks player, and a man I didn't recognize were standing there, Kon's brows lowered in a glare.

"Hey, come on in," I said, stepping aside.

"Lucy, this is Andy Morales, our team doctor, and you already know Wes and Boone."

Wes. I had forgotten his name.

Wes nodded at me and Andy shook my hand.

"He's in the family room," I said, planning to lead the way.

Kon lightly held on to my elbow to hold me back, and Wes, Boone, and Andy headed for the family room.

"How are you?" Kon asked in a hushed tone.

I shrugged. "It's going about as expected."

He put an arm around my shoulders. "You have help now. The team leaves for a road trip tomorrow, but I'm working on getting you help while I'm gone."

"I'll be okay. You don't need to do that."

His expression was grim. "You will. I have seen people go through withdrawal before, and it gets rough."

I nodded, knowing he was probably right. Though I was a person who told everyone I was fine and didn't need anything, I appreciated that Kon didn't agree.

"When someone knocks at the door, don't just open it," he said, his tone urgent. "Only open it if you know who it is."

I sighed, remembering that not only was my brother detoxing from booze cold turkey, but Nate was after me. And Kon was right—I could have been opening the door to anyone just now. I had to be smart about this.

"I'll check from now on," I assured him.

He slid his arm out from around my shoulders and put both hands on my hips. "I wish I could stay here, but I have a road trip."

My heart raced as I looked up at him, desire

swirling in his dark eyes even now. I felt it, too—a powerful urge to run upstairs with him and leave our worries behind. We couldn't, but damn, did I want to.

"Of course you have to go," I said. "But I'll be here when you get back."

"I want to see you," he said, his lips hovering above mine. "Alone."

"So do I."

"Hey guys, can you" Boone quieted, his eyes widening when he saw we were on the edge of kissing. "Shit, sorry."

"We are on the way," Kon said, not looking away from me.

Boone was already gone. Kon tightened his hold on my hips, pulling me closer until our bodies were flush.

"I have never been with a woman who is good," he murmured against my lips. "You are sweet and soft, Lucy. So good. I am burning for you."

His words made my skin tingle and my core ache with need for him. He hadn't even kissed me, but I was so turned on I couldn't think straight.

"You're good, too," I said against his lips.

He groaned. "There is a lot about me you do not know. I am not as good as you think."

I wanted him to push me up against the wall right here and kiss me. Put his hands everywhere. He was going on a road trip tomorrow and though he was right here, his body pressed to mine and his touch making me weak, I already missed him.

"You're very good to me," I said.

A couple of seconds passed, his breath warm on my lips when he said, "I want you to know who I am, but not today."

He kissed my forehead and stepped back. What did he mean? I wanted to know how Kon could be anything but the quiet, intense protective man I was falling for, but he was right that this wasn't the time.

With a soft sigh, I led the way to the family room, where Sawyer was back on the couch, Andy tightening a blood pressure cuff on his arm. He greeted me and Kon with a surly glare.

"Pressure's good," Andy said, writing something in a small notebook.

"Do you even want this for yourself?" Wes asked Sawyer.

"I've made it clear I don't."

Kon shook his head. "He does not remember what sober feels like. If he won't save his own life, we will do it for him."

"Yeah, but it's a losing battle if he's going to run to the closest bar as soon as this is over," Wes said.

"I'm not an alcoholic," Sawyer barked.

I balked. "You drink a case of beer a day and look what's happening to you from just a few hours without drinking on your usual schedule."

Wes cleared his throat. "Sawyer, you look like shit and you never leave your house. Your whole life revolves around drinking. That's alcoholism, man."

My brother looked at Boone, who nodded solemnly, and then at Andy.

"Look at it this way," Andy said gently. "If you aren't an alcoholic, quitting won't hurt at all. The more it hurts, the more you need this."

Sawyer looked down at the ground for a few seconds, then swiped his cheeks with his fingertips and turned to face me. "Okay. Let's do it."

———

SIX HOURS LATER, I was curled up at Kon's side watching a movie with some of his teammates when a loud noise and yelling upstairs made me sit upright.

"What the hell was that?" I looked at him with wide eyes.

Lars got up from his seat next to Sheridan on the love seat and walked toward the stairway. I moved to join him, but Kon held me in place with his arm.

"Boone is up there," he said. "He and Lars will take care of it."

Unfortunately, we all knew *it* was Sawyer after a full day without alcohol. I dreaded his teammates leaving for the road trip tomorrow, because they'd been taking turns sitting in Sawyer's bedroom. He was vomiting now, had a headache, and was edgy as hell.

"I'll be here tomorrow," Sheridan said, seeming to read my mind. "I can stay all day."

I gave her a grateful look. "Thank you. I need to get groceries so that will help."

"No, you will have the groceries delivered," Kon said.

I opened my mouth to object, remembered the red SUV guy, and then nodded.

"What?" Sheridan looked between us, confused. "Kon, what's it to you if she gets groceries?"

She didn't know me well, but Sheridan was still looking out for me. I liked her.

"My ex is looking for me," I said. "And if he gets to me...it won't be good."

Her expression softened. "Oh, girl. I've been there." She looked at Kon. "I'll pack a bag and stay here until you guys get back. And I'll bring my gun."

Boone walked into the room and sat down on a free chair. "What are we watching?"

"Is Sawyer okay?" I asked, getting up and walking over to Boone to see if I was seeing what I thought I was. "Did he give you a black eye?"

Boone grinned. "Yeah, that bastard's faster than I expected."

"No, you are just slower than shit," Kon said.

"Only took me one minute to get your mom in bed."

Kon's gaze darkened and he stood. "I told you no more jokes about my mother."

"How's my brother?" I asked Boone, dying to go upstairs and check on him.

Boone's expression sobered. "He's been better, but don't worry. Andy will be here soon to look in on him. And he'll need a good drywall guy because he punched a hole in his bedroom wall."

Kon took my hand and tugged on it, and I followed him back to the couch, my brow furrowed with concern.

"This is how it is," he said, putting an arm around my shoulders. "It will get better."

"And you don't have to do this alone," Sheridan said. "Sariah said she wants to come hang out tomorrow, too. She's Nash's girlfriend."

"Tough love," Kon reminded me. "We will get through this."

I knew he was right. My only regret was that I'd

waited this long to play hardball with my brother. The kind and hopeful approach I'd been employing was clearly a failure. It was time to do this Kon's way.

CHAPTER TWELVE

Kon

I HATED LEAVING Lucy to deal with Sawyer. She had Dr. Morales, Sheridan, Hadley, and Sariah helping out, but they wouldn't be much help if Nate or one of his brother's friends showed up. What if one of them pushed their way into the house? If they hurt Lucy—or anyone in our Mavericks family—I'd lose my fucking mind. Sawyer was lucid enough to at least be aware if something happened, but I wasn't sure he was in any condition to defend the girls while we were away. Especially if there was more than one attacker.

"You look like a man with a lot on his mind,"

Boone said to me as we got on the plane after kicking the snot out of the team in Boston.

We were headed to Philadelphia. We'd play there tomorrow, have a day off, and then go to Pittsburgh and Columbus after that.

Five more days until we got home.

Five days too many.

"Worried about Sawyer," I said.

"And Lucy." His eyes met mine questioningly.

I didn't respond.

"You like her," he said, no hint of humor in his voice.

"Yes." There was no point denying it after what he'd seen the other night.

"Sawyer know?"

"There is nothing to know." *Yet.*

"Looked like there was something the other night."

"It's complicated."

"Isn't it always?"

"We have to deal with Sawyer's situation," I said, hoping to redirect the conversation. I wasn't ready to talk to anyone about Lucy and me. Especially since I didn't know if there *was* a Lucy and me. We'd kissed a few times. I wanted her so badly I was jerking off twice a day, but I hadn't even taken her out on a date.

"But do you like her enough to deal with Sawyer's wrath or is this…casual?"

"I don't know," I grunted, pulling out my headphones. "I like her, but we're just friends."

"Friends don't kiss." He pointed out.

"We weren't kissing," I muttered.

He gave me a look that told me he thought I was full of shit, but apparently decided to back off. "If you say so."

Glad that conversation was over, I put my headphones on and opened my laptop, scrolling through one of the streaming services I subscribed to, looking for a movie to watch. I really didn't want to watch anything, so even though I left my headphones on, I pulled out my phone and texted Lucy.

Kon: How are things tonight?

Lucy: Sawyer's sleeping, so I just took a shower while Sheridan and Sariah hold down the fort.

Kon: Does this mean you are naked?

Lucy: Maybe. But I'll never tell. ;)

Kon: I would very much like to see this.

Lucy: I guess we'll have to work on that.

Kon: The thought of you naked is very distracting… but this is why I texted.

Lucy: You were going to ask me if I was naked?

Kon: LOL no. I was going to ask if you would like to go out on a date with me. A proper date. Just the two of us.

Away from Sawyer and the team and everything else. Maybe even go out of town or something. NOT to get naked. Just to be together. But naked would be okay also.

Lucy: LOL I'd love to go on a clothes-optional date with you. When?

Kon: We're back in five days, but there is a game the following night. What about next Wednesday?

There was a slight delay before her response.

Lucy: My schedule is clear, but it kind of depends on Sawyer. Also, what am I going to tell him?

Kon: Is going out with me going to be a problem?

Lucy: No. I'm a grown-ass woman who can date whomever I want. I just...even in his current condition, he's overprotective. And he's always been clear that he doesn't want me dating his teammates. Normally, I wouldn't give a shit, but with everything going on...

Kon: I hate to suggest something so childish, but for now maybe lie? Say you are going to spend the day with the girls?

Lucy: That's what I was thinking. I'm sure Sheridan will cover for me. Everyone is walking on eggshells around Sawyer right now, so they'll understand me not wanting to upset the applecart.

Kon: Applecart?

Lucy: It's a saying. We don't want to upset him until he's past the worst of this.

Kon: Okay. So next Wednesday?

Lucy: That sounds like heaven. Let me talk to Sheridan to see how we can work it out.

Kon: I am looking forward to this. Very much.

Lucy: Me too.

———

I WAS LACING up my skates the next night in Philadelphia when Wes sank down beside me.

"I didn't know if you'd heard the news," he said. "But Miller just got traded to Philly yesterday. He's in the lineup tonight."

I froze.

It was inevitable I'd continue to face him on the ice as long as we both played, but up until now I'd had warning. I'd somehow missed that he'd been traded to Philadelphia. And now we were going to be out there together. With me stuck in goal where he could linger and talk shit all night.

The thing was, I'd moved on and Lucy gave me something to think about beyond the darkness that lurked just beneath my well-polished exterior. As a goalie, I didn't mix it up often, and I always stayed focused. This was a distraction I didn't need.

"Kon?" Wes was waiting for me to respond.

"I'm fine," I said finally. "I don't give a shit about him. That is in the past."

"Okay. I just wanted you to know."

"Thank you." I nodded at him.

When I'd first found out about Keegan and Svetlana, I could have hurt him. My fists were considered lethal weapons back in Russia. I'd worked hard to get past that part of my life, tamp down the anger that had once driven me to violence, but it always lurked beneath the surface. The fact that I hadn't killed Keegan when I'd caught him and Svetlana in bed together said a lot about how far I'd come. I was no angel, though, and walked an emotional tightrope when it came to keeping my temper in check.

I skated onto the ice for the pregame warm-up, taking a couple of laps before pausing in front of the bench. I'd stretched in the locker room, so I didn't need to do anything else.

"You look like you're going to murder someone," Boone muttered under his breath as he stood next to me. "I'm not going to have to bail you out of jail, am I?"

"No. I am good."

"Yeah, whenever someone says that it usually means the opposite."

"Can you afford to bail me out if I am arrested?"

He paused. "Well, yeah, of course, but—"

"Then we have nothing to worry about." I gave

him a quick fist bump, hoping to lighten the mood even as he rolled his eyes at me.

Luckily, the first two periods were mostly uneventful and we were up 3–1. Keegan had smirked at me a few times, but if I got riled up every time someone smirked in hockey, we'd all be in trouble.

"How's it goin', Konstantin?" he asked, coming up on my right as we waited for the commercial break to end. No one ever used my full first name, so he was definitely up to something.

I ignored him but could practically feel my blood pressure amping up.

I was determined not to let him get to me.

Life was good.

I'd met someone special.

Things were still early for Lucy and me, but there was no mistaking the spark between us. The last thing I wanted was to slide down memory lane with Keegan fucking Miller.

"Did you know your ex-fiancée was a prostitute?" Keegan taunted, just loud enough for me to hear.

I took a pull from my water bottle, wondering how the fuck he'd found that out. Svetlana and I had never told a soul about our pasts. Despite what she'd done, I would never betray her like that. And no one had a right to say a fucking word about how we'd survived.

"You did know," Keegan continued, finally making eye contact with me.

"You're like a small buzzing insect," I responded in Russian, knowing it would piss him off that he couldn't understand me. "The kind I could squish under my boot."

"Fuck you." He skated away as the linesman got ready to drop the puck but I was nervous.

Not for myself, but I didn't know for sure whether or not Svetlana had made it home to Russia. If Keegan was talking about her past publicly, it could impact her ability to stay in the US. Immigration could be tricky for someone like her.

The next face-off in our zone had Keegan off to my left and he immediately started running his mouth.

"Were you her pimp?" Keegan asked, inching closer to me. "Did you watch other guys fuck her? Was that how you got your kicks when you weren't in the ring?"

Jesus. Fucking. Christ.

What the hell had Svetlana told him?

"You know that's why I dumped her skanky ass, right?" he continued, as if we weren't in the middle of a game.

"She got herself pregnant. Like I was going to marry a fucking whore."

Pregnant.

"You should shut your fucking mouth before I shut it for you," I growled, thankful for the game to start back up. It felt like we'd had a million commercial breaks and icing calls that had stopped the action and given him time to fuck with my head.

When one of his teammates hit a slap shot over my right shoulder to bring them within one goal, I mentally grimaced.

"Shake it off," Wes said, skating over to me. "Miller talking shit?"

I grunted.

"You want to jump him in the hotel parking lot after the game, I'm in. But you've got to hang on for six more minutes. You hear me?"

I nodded.

I turned and faced the net, away from everyone getting ready for the next face-off. I took a cleansing breath and pictured that last puck going into my glove instead of the net, reminding myself what I would do next time. I lifted my mask and squirted a shot of water onto my face, then shook it out onto the ice in front of me. I focused on one tiny drop, slowly freezing on the ice, and centered myself.

Now I was ready.

I slid my mask back down and turned around. I positioned myself on the goal line, right in the middle of the net and watched the puck drop. Philly's star forward grabbed it and headed in my direction with Keegan flanking him on the right. The first shot hit the post but Keegan picked it up behind me and came around front, passing it back to his teammate, who took another quick shot I stopped easily. The ref blew the whistle, but Keegan kept coming, knocking me back and trying to work the puck out of my glove.

I managed to flip onto my stomach, keeping my glove and the puck beneath me. Lars shoved Keegan off me and I turned over just as five or six guys from both teams all came together, gloves and fists flying. The linesmen and ref were in the middle, trying to separate everyone, but it was hard to see what was happening. I got to my feet as two guys went after Lars. He was a big motherfucker, but Philly's guys weren't exactly small. I nudged the one closest to me, kicking at his skate to keep him off balance. Before I had a chance to do anything else, Keegan was in my face.

"You wanna go, asshole?" Keegan had already dropped his gloves, holding up his fists.

This guy was truly stupid.

Then he proved it by shoving me.

"Come on, you Russian fuck. Whatcha got? You know you're dying to show off how you can fight. Svetlana told me how you like to hurt people."

I didn't know why she would have told him anything, but I was willing to bet my left nut she hadn't said *that*. My gloves came off before I could stop myself, a cross between amusement and annoyance ripping through me. But I wouldn't hit him first. I'd let him take the first punch.

Then I'd end it.

As expected, he swung his fist but it barely glanced off my jaw.

"Is this all?" I asked patiently. I knew this was being filmed, so Coach and every hockey fan watching would see that I didn't start it.

"You want more?" He swung again, hitting me twice, once with each fist, but I barely felt the blows. This guy had no idea what underground fighting was like in Russia if he thought he could hurt me like this.

I smiled just before using my right fist for an uppercut under his jaw that I knew would jar his teeth and get him off balance. I followed it up with a jab to the left side of his face that took him down.

He moaned but wasn't getting up.

The ref and linesmen were blowing their whistles, Lars was punching the shit out of one of Philly's enforcers, and Nash was trying to pull two guys off of Wes. I was surrounded by chaos but felt strangely calm.

I was over Svetlana romantically, but Keegan was the scum of the earth. It was one thing for her to cheat on me—there was no way for us to be together after that—but I still felt responsible for her. I wouldn't be alive if she hadn't sacrificed herself for me. So despite her infidelity, I didn't begrudge her moving on. She was broken, probably more than I was, and I needed her to find peace. Maybe even love. If for no other reason than to assuage my guilty conscience.

Keegan had used her. Once he'd succeeded in breaking us up, he'd apparently kept her around long enough to knock her up and then kicked her to the curb.

And I fucking hated him for it.

It was that simple.

CHAPTER THIRTEEN

Lucy

"This bread is the reason my first wife married me," Luigi said as he held up a loaf of cinnamon bread.

His brother snorted from the other side of the front counter. "That tracks. It sure as hell wasn't for your looks or personality."

"At least I found a woman who wanted to marry me," Luigi countered.

"Yeah, *three* of 'em," Mario shot back. "And those two divorces were messy. No thank you. I'll be a bachelor for life. Master of my own remote control."

Luigi rolled his eyes and gestured at his brother with his thumb. "Lucy, that's what you call making virtue of necessity. This guy couldn't find a woman to marry him if he stood on the corner with a bagful of cash."

"Dad, she just wants to buy some bread," the young woman who had helped me last time cut in. "You don't need to give her your life story."

I smiled at Luigi. "I don't mind."

It was the truth. I looked forward to my early morning visits to Morelli Brothers. Sawyer was still at home sleeping, and I was a bundle of nervous energy over my date with Kon later, so I'd decided to make a big breakfast this morning. Sheridan was coming over later and I knew she loved bacon, so I was stocking up on bacon, eggs, and the ingredients for French toast casserole.

"This will make the French toast of your dreams," Luigi assured me. "Is this for Mr. Italian Beef?"

"I don't think he'll be over early enough to eat it. Mostly it's for my brother and a friend."

Luigi nodded his approval. "You hear that, Maria? Lucy's not shacking up with her boyfriend."

Maria ignored him.

"He's not my boyfriend," I clarified. "We're just going out on our first date tonight."

Luigi gave me a pointed look. "But you won't shack up with him, will you? He'll never buy the cow if you give him the milk for free."

"I'm not a cow, Dad," Maria said as she wiped down a counter.

I didn't want to get in the middle of this family conversation, so I gave Luigi a bright smile and said, "I'll take a loaf of the cinnamon bread and a half dozen brownies."

"You got it, kid."

He rang up my order and I paid him with my debit card. As he passed me my bag, he peered at me over the rim of his glasses.

"Don't let Mr. Italian Beef get handsy on the first date now," he said. "A peck on the cheek is enough."

Mario snorted out a laugh, shaking his head. "Don't listen to him, Lucy. His son Anthony was conceived on a first date."

"That was…a unique situation," Luigi said.

"Enjoy your date, Lucy," Maria said. "Where are you guys going?"

"I'm not sure."

She grinned. "You'll have to tell us all about it."

"Definitely."

———

"THANKS AGAIN FOR BREAKFAST," Sheridan said a few hours later. "I'll meet you at that little coffee shop at two."

She stopped on her walk to the door that led from the garage into the kitchen, making sure Sawyer wasn't looking at her, and then gave me a theatrically dramatic wink.

"See you then," I said, smiling.

After she left, Sawyer sighed heavily from his seat at the kitchen table. "That was amazing, but I ate way too much."

"It's a good day for a run," I suggested.

"It's like twenty-five degrees outside, Luce."

"So wear a jacket."

He got up and carried his plate over to the sink. "I'm in no shape for running."

It had been almost a week since his last drink. The physical symptoms of alcohol withdrawal had passed, but the craving for alcohol was still there. I was trying to fill the void by cooking good meals for him, but I was going to have to wean him back onto healthier food soon.

"Hey, what's up with you and Kon?" he asked, leaning against the counter and crossing his arms.

I feigned surprise. "What do you mean?"

"Cut the shit."

Crap. Was I that bad of a liar?

I shrugged. "I think he's nice. He's helped me a lot since I got here."

"I know there's something going on; don't bullshit me. I heard you guys were getting cozy on the couch the other night."

"I mean, we sat close together, but we were fully clothed. Your teammates were in the room with us. It wasn't a big deal."

"Just be careful. Kon's a good guy, but he's nothing like the guys you're used to dating."

I laughed bitterly. "That's a good thing. Nate ended up not being the friendly neighborhood insurance agent he seemed like."

"Kon's intense. There's no one better to have on your side, but…" He looked away.

"What?"

Sawyer sighed. "His last girlfriend cheated on him with one of our teammates. Remember that fight he got into during the game we watched on TV the other night?"

"Yeah?"

"That's the guy Svetlana cheated on him with. Keegan."

"Oh."

It made more sense now. Kon wasn't just pissed off about hockey, but about his former girlfriend. Was he still hung up on her? Clearly there were unresolved feelings of some kind.

A flare of jealousy rose in my chest. If Kon liked women who treated him like garbage, I'd be a disappointment.

"Just be careful, okay?" Sawyer said.

"I will."

KON WORE the black jeans I liked on him, this time with tennis shoes, a plain gray hoodie, and a black leather jacket. A table of two women stared at him as he walked past, his gaze focused entirely on me.

"Hi," he said, kissing me on the cheek.

Shit. He smelled amazing. How was I supposed to be careful around him when he smelled like that?

"Hey."

"Did you get here okay? No problems from Sawyer?"

I shrugged. "One of your teammates told him we were cozy on the couch the other night, so he thinks there's something between us."

A smile played on Kon's lips. "I know. He sent me about twenty texts warning me to stay away from you."

"What did you say?"

"I told him he was overreacting." He reached for my hand. "Want to get coffee to go?"

I looked at the chalkboard menu. "If you want to get a coffee, I'll get a hot chocolate."

We stood in line for a couple of minutes, and he only let go of my hand when he needed to get his wallet to pay for our drinks.

As soon as we were in his car, I put my drink in a cup holder, took a deep breath, and dove right in.

"Do you still have feelings for your ex?"

He looked over at me. "Feelings of wanting to be with her? No."

I nodded. Kon put the car back in park.

"What do you want to know?" he asked me.

There was no tension or anger in his tone. It sounded like a straightforward offer to ask any questions I wanted to ask about her. That seemed... unusually emotionally healthy.

"I know we're just having fun here," I said. "And I'm leaving eventually. So I don't really have a right to ask anything."

"Ask me, Lucy."

God, I liked him. There were no games. I wished I could have met him at a different time and place in my life.

"Do you miss her?"

I could tell he was seriously considering my question before answering. "I miss having someone, but no, I do not miss her."

"What's she like?"

"Svetlana? She is…moody. Demanding. Very strong."

My heart raced as I held his gaze. "I'm not moody or demanding. I'm not sure about strong."

"You have to be strong to survive in Russia. And I like you, Lucy, just the way you are. Svetlana and I did not work out, and I have moved on."

I nodded and covered his hand with mine. "Okay. Thank you. Let's go have some fun."

Smiling, he backed out of his parking space and started driving.

"Where are we going?" I asked him.

"I have dinner reservations at six. And until then, how about the art museum?"

"That sounds great."

On the drive, he told me about a trip he had taken to an art museum in Russia with his grandma, his eyes lighting up at the memory.

"It was filled with treasures," he said. "Crowns and carriages. Things I could not have imagined until I saw them. My grandma cried because she'd never seen anything so beautiful."

"Was it her first time visiting there?"

He nodded. "We could never have afforded a trip to Moscow before I started fighting."

"Fighting?"

He nodded, his expression grim. "I fought to

make money. It wasn't that I enjoyed it, but that we needed the money."

From his tone, I sensed that he thought I wouldn't approve of him fighting.

"I understand," I said gently. "I admire you for doing what you had to do to take care of your family."

When we got to the museum, we walked hand in hand, admiring most of the art but occasionally laughing at our modern take on historical paintings.

"I feel this," I said as we stood in front of a painting of a woman swooning on a couch, one of her breasts hanging out of her dress. "It's me when I take off my bra."

Kon laughed and gave me a questioning look.

"Underwire is a prison," I said.

"I will take yours off anytime," he said, his grin wicked.

I was already hoping he'd take me to his place after dinner. Detoxing Sawyer had been stressful, and I worried every day about what was going to happen with Nate. It was nice to leave those things behind, just for today, and focus only on the dark, sexy Russian offering to take my bra off.

When I looked up at him, unable to keep from smiling, he cupped my cheek and kissed me softly. It was another one of those moments where nothing existed but the two of us.

"We have to get to dinner," he said against my lips.

"Maybe we can continue this later," I murmured.

"Yes. We will eat quickly."

He took my hand and we headed for his car, parked in a nearby parking garage. The restaurant he'd reserved a table at was only about fifteen minutes from the museum, and the host lit up when he saw Kon walking in.

"Mr. Volkov, welcome back. We've reserved our best table for you."

The restaurant had dim lighting, candles flickering at the center of every table. The host took our coats and immediately poured me a glass of wine from the bottle chilling on the table.

"Your usual, Mr. Volkov?" he asked Kon.

"Please."

"Very good, sir."

As soon as the host walked away, I gave Kon a puzzled look. "Do you come here a lot?"

"I do actually. I love the food. It's almost as good as yours."

I laughed and shook my head. "You don't have to flatter me."

"I'm being honest. I love your cooking."

I warmed at his compliment. "Thank you. I've always loved cooking."

"What are your plans for tomorrow?"

I sighed. "I bought the stuff to cook for me and Sawyer, because he still hasn't decided if he wants to go to Wes and Hadley's house yet for Thanksgiving."

"Was he okay today?"

"He was. He's eating more and feeling better every day. I think the worst might be behind us."

"I hope so."

Our server had just arrived at the table with Kon's drink and a basket of bread when Kon's phone rang. He glanced at the screen and grimaced.

"Boone. I need to answer."

"I'll come back," the server said, leaving.

Boone was at Sawyer's house, watching him for the evening. I held my breath as Kon spoke to him.

"For how long?" He groaned. "Okay…no, don't do that…we're on our way."

He hung up the phone and met my gaze across the table. "Sawyer locked himself in the bathroom with a bottle of something, but Boone doesn't know what. He asked if he should break down the door but I said no."

"Oh my god." I got up from my seat, grabbed my bag, and headed for the door, my coat forgotten.

So much for the worst being behind us.

CHAPTER FOURTEEN

Kon

Sawyer was still locked in the bathroom when we got home, and I hung back with Boone as Lucy ran forward, lightly knocking on the door.

"Sawyer? It's me. Please open the door."

To my surprise, Sawyer opened the door as soon as she asked.

He looked…defeated. That was the only word I could think of. He wasn't as pale anymore, his hair was freshly washed, and his face clean-shaven, but the look in his eyes was something I'd seen before. And it was devastating for me to see it in my good-hearted, strong, athletic friend.

"Sawyer?" Lucy must have sensed it too as she

pulled the unopened bottle of Jack Daniels from his hand. "What happened? What's wrong? You didn't have any Jack, did you?"

"No." He shook his head and then leaned against the wall, slumping down a little.

"Then why the fuck wouldn't you come out for me?" Boone demanded, scowling.

"You guys don't get it." He looked from one to the other, letting out a heavy sigh.

"What don't we get?" Lucy asked gently.

"It's not that I'm an alcoholic. I'm not. I don't have an addictive personality. Yeah, I'd been drinking so much my body had a reaction when I stopped, but this isn't about not being *able* to stop. It's about not wanting to. Losing Annie wasn't just the loss of my life partner and soul mate—it's like my reason for living is gone. I truly couldn't give a shit about hockey, my future, none of it. If it wasn't for Nate threatening you, Luce, I would've already been drinking again. And that's the only reason I didn't start up again tonight."

"Sawyer." Lucy looked as heartbroken as I felt, but I didn't know what to say.

"This pain, the hole in my life since Annie's been gone, is never going away." Sawyer looked away, as if it embarrassed him to say that. "So neither will my need to drink, because that's the only time I don't feel it." He waved a hand as Lucy started to say something. "Please don't. Okay? I'm fine. I'm not going to drink. I'm not going to do anything. Not now anyway. I appreciate all of you, but I'm not the man I used to be. And the sooner you come to terms with that, the easier it will be all around."

"Sawyer, you have friends who care about you. A lucrative career. *Me*." She gave him a sweet smile. "You have a lot more to live for than you think. And one day—"

"Please don't do that. I can't think about what might happen someday. I can barely figure out what's happening today."

"Fine." Lucy lifted her chin, changing tactics. "How about tomorrow? Are we going to Wes and Hadley's?"

"You can. I have no desire to be around a bunch of people, especially people who knew Annie." He motioned impatiently. "Look, I'm going to bed. Sorry I messed up your evening." He gave me a pointed look that told me he knew damn well Lucy hadn't been out with Sheridan.

Then he turned and disappeared up the stairs, the click of his bedroom door closing coming a few seconds later.

"Fuck." Boone held up his hands. "I don't even know what the fuck to say to all that."

"There's nothing to say," I said quietly. "He will eventually move past the grief, but I think it will take a long time."

"Sawyer used to drink like a fish in college," Lucy said after a moment. "And he never had a problem. So while I think his drinking was a lot more serious this time, I also believe that he's in control enough to know what he's doing. Which is almost sadder than him being an addict."

"This is fucking exhausting," Boone muttered, moving toward the living room. "I'm here for him. I'm not complaining. It's just draining to see him like this, knowing there's nothing we can do. And I fucking hate feeling helpless."

"Same." Lucy sank onto the couch and leaned back.

I sat beside her, sliding an arm around her shoulders. I didn't give a shit if Boone saw us together; he wouldn't say anything.

"He won't go to therapy, right?" Boone asked. "Or some kind of support group for widows and widowers?"

Lucy shook her head. "Nope. Won't even discuss it. Said he doesn't care about other people's grief, that he can't even deal with his own."

"All we can do is continue to support him," I said. "At some point, he has to *want* to start to live again. I do not know if he has hit rock bottom or not."

We were all quiet for a few minutes.

"If you guys are good, I'm going to head out," Boone said finally. "I was going to meet up with Rory and a few of the guys, maybe get a few beers."

"Go." Lucy waved a hand. "I'm fine. I'm going to start prepping the food for tomorrow, I guess."

"I will stay," I told her, since I had no intention of cutting our evening this short. "I can help."

"Would you guys want to eat with us tomorrow?" she asked slowly, looking at me and then at Boone. "I think I might lose my mind if it's just Sawyer and me sitting down for Thanksgiving dinner. It's depressing enough on regular days, much less a holiday."

"Of course." I wrapped my hand around hers. "Whatever you need."

"You sure you want an extra mouth to feed?" Boone asked dubiously.

"Are you kidding? I bought a sixteen-pound turkey. We're going to have leftovers for days. And honestly, I need as many distractions as possible because watching Sawyer give up on life is killing me."

"Then I'll be here," Boone said softly. "Just tell me what time."

"Any time after two. We'll probably have football on and eat around four."

"See you then."

I didn't know what to say once Boone left. Our evening had been interrupted and there was no doubt Lucy was struggling with Sawyer's situation.

"What can I do?" I whispered, nuzzling her neck.

She leaned into me, her eyes searching mine. "Kiss me?"

"Yes. I can do this."

I cupped the back of her neck with my hand and pulled her to me. Her lips yielded to mine like they were made for me. I gently pushed my tongue between them and began to stroke in and out. She tasted amazing, like sugar and honey and sex. Her fingers curled into my shirt, drawing me even closer, and she moaned as I deepened the kiss. She all but melted into my chest and I stroked my hands down the curvy globes of her ass, squeezing hard enough to make her moan again. They were a perfect hand-ful, and I imagined slapping them while taking her from behind.

This time I was the one who groaned.

I sank onto the couch and tugged her down so she was on my lap, straddling me. I was already sporting the boner of the decade, my dick throbbing painfully as she ground her crotch into mine. I slid my hands through her thick, silky hair.

"You're beautiful, Lucy."

"Th-thanks." Her voice was a breathy whisper, her eyes glassy and half-closed.

I kissed her again, probably a little more roughly than I intended, but I was dying inside. It had been a long time since I'd wanted someone this much. Our tongues were hot, doing a sexy dance that had me close to embarrassing myself. She wanted me too, I could feel it, but I also didn't want to rush things. It somehow felt important to take my time with her. Lucy was not a woman whose feelings you toyed with.

My lips trailed across her cheek to the soft spot behind her ear. I nibbled there and then gently nipped at the skin, following it up with strokes of my tongue. She shivered beneath me, and I realized we were going to get carried away if I didn't stop this. I wanted her, but not like this, and definitely not where Sawyer could potentially walk in on us. I hated feeling like a teenager, sneaking around so my date's parents wouldn't catch us. We didn't have much choice tonight, so I regretfully pulled away.

"Sweetheart…" My voice cracked a little as I tried to tamp down the lust coursing through my veins. "I want you. Very much. But not here. Not now."

She sighed. "No, of course not. You're right."

"Soon," I whispered. "Sawyer knows we were together tonight, so I don't think we have to hide if we go out again."

"If?" Her eyes twinkled as she cocked her head.

"When." I leaned forward and kissed the tip of her nose.

"You're leaving on a road trip Friday, right?"

I nodded.

"Damn."

"Short this time, just three days. And when I return, we will have a...what do you call it? Do-over?"

She laughed. "Yes."

I rested my hands on her hips, loving how it felt to have her in my lap.

"Do you need help in the kitchen?" I asked finally.

"I think I'm going to make pumpkin pies," she said. "Do you like those?"

"Yes. This is an American tradition I enjoy."

"Then you should enjoy watching me make it." She got to her feet and held out her hands. She playfully pulled me up and I wrapped my arms around her.

"I enjoy everything when we are together," I said quietly, looking deep into her eyes.

She bit her lower lip, gazing up at me. "I do too."

I brushed her hair away from her face and leaned down to kiss her again. Her lips were addictive, calling to me every time I looked at her. This was going to be a problem tomorrow with Sawyer and Boone underfoot all day.

"If you keep this up," she whispered breathlessly, "I may have to take you upstairs and have my way with you."

I groaned. "This is very tempting, but maybe we should stick to baking tonight. I do not want Sawyer to try to kill me."

She giggled, a sweet, lighthearted sound that made me want to hear her do it more often.

"I'll protect you," she said, sashaying into the kitchen and leaving me drooling after her delectable backside.

CHAPTER FIFTEEN

Lucy

"THOSE ARE STILL REALLY HOT," I cautioned as Sawyer speared a sausage ball with a toothpick and raised it to his mouth.

"Shit." His eyes widened and he chewed quickly. "That burned my mouth."

"If only you'd known it was hot."

After swallowing, he gave me a look. "It's already one fifteen, Luce. I'm starving."

Blowing a strand of hair that had escaped my ponytail from my face, I glared at him. Stabbing a man who was demanding while someone was trying to cook an entire Thanksgiving spread alone had to be a reduced charge of manslaughter. If I could get a female judge, I'd probably only get probation.

"I'm cooking as fast as I can!" I raged. "I just put two appetizers out, and if you'll give them a fucking minute to cool down then you can eat them."

Kon was there, putting his hands on my shoulders. "You are doing great, Lucy. How can we help?"

"You guys could work on the corn casserole."

"Touchdown!" Boone shouted from the family room. "Let's fucking go, boys!"

Sawyer took off, not looking back. Kon tried to pretend he didn't want to, but I could see the longing in his eyes.

"You can go watch football," I said. "I've got this covered."

"No, I want to help."

I smiled and kissed him. "You're the best, thank you. I promise I've got it covered. I just needed that little meltdown and now I'll be fine."

"This feels like a trick," he said, his brow furrowed.

I laughed. "I'll let you know if I need help, okay?"

He glanced at my wineglass. "I will refill that before I go."

"Perfect."

I regretted telling my mom not to come. She'd been eager to find help with her sister and make the trip, but not knowing where we'd be with Sawyer's sobriety, I'd told her not to. And of course, being me, I'd taken on too much with this meal. The kitchen counters were covered in dishes.

"I've got this," I assured myself softly. "Just one dish at a time."

But that was tricky if I wanted everything to be done—and hot—at the same time. I'd never cooked Thanksgiving dinner for a man I was interested in, and I wanted everything to be just right.

I put a Bruno Mars album on shuffle on my phone and started chopping. I'd gotten through the onions and was starting the celery for the stuffing when someone knocked on the front door.

The hairs on the back of my neck stood up. Someone was here on Thanksgiving? That didn't feel right.

Kon and Sawyer both stalked out of the family room, their expressions solemn. Though I doubted Nate or whoever he had sent to watch me was knocking on the front door, I appreciated how much they both wanted to protect me.

The yell I heard when they answered the door sounded like a victory cry. I washed my hands to go see what was going on, but before I made it to the doorway, Lars walked through it, wearing oven mitts on each hand, and carrying a casserole dish.

"I have buffalo chicken mac and cheese," the giant defender said.

I stared at him dumbly for a second before saying, "Um, okay."

Hadley and Wes were right behind him. I'd only spent a little time with Hadley, but she embraced me like we were old friends.

"Hey, girl," she said. "So sorry to crash your Thanksgiving, but my stubborn husband decided about an hour ago that if Sawyer wouldn't come to us, we were coming to him."

"Oh." Panic filled my chest as the room filled with people. "Okay."

I didn't have enough food, enough chairs, or enough plates. This was going to be a disaster.

"Don't freak out," Hadley said. "We brought a ton of food. I had a bunch of things catered and I made a bunch myself, and everyone brought stuff. We brought a giant ham, two turkeys, and a ton of ribs."

She was right. Everyone who walked into the room had something in hand, and the counters were filling up.

Sheridan was laughing when she approached me for a hug. "It'll be fine, I promise. We've got paper plates and extra chairs, and more food than you can imagine."

I met Kon's gaze across the room, and he winked

at me. People I hadn't met yet introduced themselves, some of them telling me whether the dish they'd brought needed to be kept cold or warm until we ate.

By the time the room cleared, I was in a daze. Sawyer was setting up the football game on the TV in the basement, which was bigger and also had a bar the guys could congregate at. The platter of sausage balls was empty. But somehow, I had a feeling this was all going to work out.

They'd *moved* Thanksgiving for my brother. I loved that his team was a family, looking out for each other and not asking for permission to do it.

"Want me to finish chopping this?" Sariah asked, picking up the knife on the cutting board with a pile of celery next to it.

"Sure, that would be great. Thanks."

I walked into the family room to see if we needed to bring in extra chairs, but people were just sitting on the floor. Kids were bouncing from lap to lap.

"What's that?" a little girl asked me, pointing to the wall of photos behind the couch.

It was Nash's dick pic. My jaw dropped and I gave Sheridan a panicked look.

"Annalise, Uncle Lars wants you to come play in the basement," she said.

Annalise's face lit up and she ran, Sheridan

asking someone to move from the couch so she could scoop the offending picture from the wall.

I just laughed because what else could I do? Annalise ran back into the room a few seconds later, breathless.

"Excuse me, where is the basement?" she asked.

"I'll take you," I said.

She took my hand as we walked to the basement door, melting my heart.

"Horseshit!" someone yelled as we walked down the stairs.

Annalise looked up at me. "That means the refs are making bad calls."

I wasn't sure whose daughter she was, but this little girl was something. It was so easy to imagine her wrapping anyone around her little finger.

"Uncle Lars, let's play," she said, running toward Lars as soon as she saw him.

He smiled, picking her up when she reached him.

The Mavericks players were spread out over the couches and standing at the bar. I scanned the faces there, worried I'd see Sawyer with a drink in hand. He wasn't there, though.

When I finally found him, Sawyer was in the kitchen loading up a plate with appetizers.

"Doing alright?" he asked me.

"Yeah, I'm good."

Kon approached us, putting his hand on my hip. "What do you need us to help with, Lucy?"

"You can start by getting your hand off her," Sawyer said with a scowl.

Kon's gaze darkened as he stared down my brother, not moving his hand.

"Guys, let's not do this right now," I said softly.

Kon's body relaxed and he nodded. "You are right."

"I need you guys to get the extra tables and chairs set up. Hopefully we can have a chair for everyone when it's time to eat."

Sawyer shrugged. "Okay, but don't sweat it hard, Luce. People can sit on the couches to eat, too."

I nodded, my gaze landing on the antique sideboard Annie had found in San Francisco when she and Sawyer were traveling. She'd had it stripped and refinished, and it was massive enough to hold a lot of food.

"Go ahead and clear everything off that sideboard, too," I told them.

"The what?" Sawyer gave me a puzzled look.

I pointed at it. "That big piece of white furniture over there."

"Ah, gotcha."

"Actually…" I eyed an empty wall. "If you guys

could move it over there, we could fit a table and chairs where it is now."

"I'll get Lars to help me move it," Sawyer said.

Kon glared at him. "I can help you move it."

"That thing's a fucking beast. Your little goalie muscles can't handle it, trust me."

Kon scoffed. "You have not lifted anything heavier than a beer can in months."

Sawyer flexed. "Still rock solid, baby. If we need any flying pucks caught, we'll give you a call."

He was being obnoxious, but this was the most energy I'd seen out of Sawyer since before Annie died. I covertly took Kon's hand in mine and gave it a squeeze, silently asking him to give in on this one.

"I will set up the tables and chairs," Kon said.

"Hey, Ross brought his grandparents if you need some help," Sawyer quipped.

As soon as he was out of earshot, Kon gave me a look of annoyance. "I like him better drunk."

"No, you don't. He's just being an ass about us going out on a date."

His grin was wicked. "I could sleep over tonight. Stay in your room with you."

"One of you would end up with a broken nose."

"Him, obviously. He has a beer belly. Sawyer could not outrun a sloth right now."

I gave him a pleading look. "Don't kick him when he's down, okay?"

He immediately looked remorseful. "You are right. If it makes you happy, I will be his punching bag. For now."

"Thank you."

He kissed me and gave me a reassuring squeeze.

"You are good?" he asked.

"I'm good. Go watch football. But set up the tables and chairs first, please."

With a grin, he nodded. I went back to the meal prep, Hadley passing me a glass as I walked over.

"Looks like you're one of us now," she said, holding her own glass up for a cheers.

I clinked my glass against hers and took a sip. "Oh wow, that's amazing. What is this?"

"Turkey punch," she said, giving me a conspiratorial smile. "I switch up the recipe every year, but it's always got a high enough alcohol content to make the stress of hosting feel fun." She looked down at her stomach. "There's also an unleaded version for those who can't partake."

My eyes widened as I gave her a questioning look. "Wait, are you…?"

"Yup. We're adding another inmate to our asylum."

Sheridan and Sariah approached, both with glasses in hand, and we all clinked glasses again.

"I'm going to start putting food in Crock-Pots to keep it warm," Hadley said after we'd all taken a sip of our drinks. "And the caterers gave me a bunch of warmers, too."

We all got to work, and Sariah bumped her hip against mine as we chopped veggies together.

"So, you and Konstantin, huh?" she said, grinning.

"Kind of?" I said, looking behind me to make sure no one was listening. "It's still early, but…it's good. I like him."

"He's nuts about you," Sheridan said.

"You think?"

She laughed. "Girl, I know. I've never seen him all snuggly with a woman like he is with you, asking them if they're good and offering to help…in the kitchen."

"He's very sweet," I said, warming inside.

"He's sweet to you, but not anyone else," Hadley said in a low voice. "Did you guys see what he did to Keegan Miller in that game the other night? He broke his nose."

"He deserved it," Sheridan said, giving me a questioning look. "Do you know about what happened between the two of them?"

"Yes. I can't imagine what that was like for Kon."

Sariah shrugged. "The trash took itself out. He deserves better."

As if on cue, he came into the kitchen, walking over to me and putting a hand on my hip.

"Tables and chairs are done. What else do you need?"

"Not a thing," I said, looking at him over my shoulder.

He smiled and gave me a quick kiss. "Tell me if you need anything, okay?"

"I will."

As soon as he was out of the room, the other women laughed lightly.

"Yeah, he's an absolute goner," Hadley said.

CHAPTER SIXTEEN

Kon

I'D SPENT Thanksgivings with teammates every year since I'd come to America. I'd been twenty that first year, Svetlana twenty-one, and neither of us had spoken enough English to be social. My last team hadn't tried that hard to get to know us, but the moment I'd gotten to St. Louis, it had been like finding long-lost brothers. I hadn't shown much emotion back then, and still didn't show much now, but I felt it. Even Svetlana had noticed the change in me, when I'd begun talking about my teammates and their significant others, suggesting we start attending team barbeques and other events. She'd always said no, and deep down, that had been the beginning of the end for us.

Looking back, I was sure she'd been jealous. I wanted to make a new life here and put the pain of the past and Russia behind me. But I had a job, success, and friends. She was alone most of the time, self-conscious about not speaking English and unwilling to go to school to learn. I'd bought her a subscription to an online learning program for Christmas one year, but she'd never bothered to try it out. At some point, I'd started leaving her at home and started spending more time with my teammates. I had no doubt that was how she'd ended up with Keegan.

Lucy was completely different. Not just because she was American and related to Sawyer, but because she was genuinely having fun. She wasn't faking it or hanging on to me for attention. She was comfortable in her own skin, no matter where we were, and I enjoyed the way she fit in. No one had ever made Svetlana feel bad about her English pronunciations, but she'd used it as a crutch. I still didn't speak perfect English, but I had no problem having conversations and relationships with these people.

I could suddenly picture myself with Lucy long term, the two of us hanging out with the team, at home, traveling. I'd barely taken her out on a date, we hadn't been intimate, and yet, I could see it in my mind's eye. She was already important to me, and I was suddenly overwhelmed with need. To be alone with her, talk to her, touch her.

God, I really fucking needed to touch her.

I went looking for her after we'd eaten several times, had dessert twice, and took the kids outside to play tag for an hour. I found her in the kitchen, putting away leftovers.

"You have done too much today," I whispered against her ear, wrapping my arms around her from behind. "You are a lovely hostess, but you also deserve to relax and enjoy the day."

She leaned back against me. "Thank you. I will."

I pressed a light kiss on the side of her neck. "I have not kissed you all day."

She turned in my arms, lifting to her toes and pressing her lips to mine. A spark ignited and I couldn't help but deepen the kiss, sliding my tongue between her lips. I let my hands drift down her back until I got to the bottom of the long sweater she wore. I skimmed my hand up her side until I reached the bare skin of her waist. She was soft and warm, her body close to mine as our mouths practically made love.

Maybe that was corny, but it was the only way to

describe what was happening here. Tongues tangling, gliding in and out, very similar to what I would do to her once we were in bed.

"Come home with me," I whispered against her lips. "Stay the night."

"Yes." Her blue eyes burned bright with desire.

"You two should take this party somewhere more...private." Sheridan's voice was laced with humor as she came into the kitchen, hands laden with empty dishes.

"Can you make sure someone sticks around until late to keep an eye on Sawyer?" Lucy asked her. "Kon and I were just talking about...leaving."

Sheridan nodded. "Absolutely. Go on and get out of here while he's absorbed in all things football. And I'll make sure everything is settled here before we leave."

"Oh, you don't have to—" Lucy began.

"Go already!" Sheridan made a shooing motion at us.

"Just bring what you'll need for the night," I said to Lucy. "We'll come back early tomorrow since I have practice."

"Okay." She winked before turning and running up the stairs.

———

I HADN'T THOUGHT I would have company tonight, so there were dishes in the kitchen sink, and I hadn't made my bed this morning, but my weekly cleaning service kept things from getting too messy. Besides, I didn't think Lucy cared much about the state of my apartment because the moment we got inside I wrapped my arms around her and kissed the top of her head.

"Sorry it's a mess," I whispered, kissing a trail down her neck to her shoulder. "I didn't think you would end up here tonight."

"As long as there's no wet spot on the bed, I'm good."

I frowned. "Wet spot? You mean, like from sex with another woman? No way. I bring no one to my home. Ever."

"That's nice." She looked around as I closed my fingers around hers.

"Do you want a tour? The condo is not so big."

"Sure."

I showed her the kitchen, the open-concept living area, and the two guest rooms. My condo was expensive and modern, but I hadn't done much in the way of decorating since I spent most of my time in bed or on the couch watching TV.

I left my room for last, planning to go back to the living room once she saw it, but she had other ideas.

"Your bed is *massive*." She gave me a flirty smile, wiggling her eyebrows.

"I like to stretch out," I said, smiling back at her. "I didn't bring you here for sex, Lucy. I want to spend time with you, even if we just talk and cuddle."

"So...sex is off the table?" Her eyes danced with mischief as she slowly tugged off her sweater.

"This is *not* what I said," I murmured, pulling her against me. "I want to spend time with you. Alone. Away from...everyone. We are always surrounded. But I also want to be a gentleman."

"Are you a romantic, Konstantin?" she asked, wrapping her arms around my neck.

I loved the way she said my full name. "I would like to be. For you. If you like that."

"I like romance," she whispered, leaning up on her toes so her lips were a breath away from mine. "But I also like sex. I want you, Konstantin. We've waited long enough."

I wanted to take things slow, add romance and tenderness to our first time together, but the feel of her full breasts against my chest and my own aching need overrode my good intentions. I pressed my mouth to hers and slid my tongue inside, anxious to taste her. I nibbled and explored until I couldn't hold back anymore and dove deeper. She was right there with me, her soft, warm body molded to mine as we kissed and kissed and kissed.

"Shirt." She panted, breaking away and tugging at my Henley.

I yanked it over my head, dropping it to the ground and watching as she crawled onto the bed, crooking her finger at me to follow, which I did without hesitation. I loved how she was taking the lead, showing me what she wanted.

But now it was my turn.

"Too many clothes," I said, pulling her leggings down and tossing them to the side before yanking off my jeans.

She wore a matching bra and panty set, made of sheer white lace, with tiny bows between her breasts and on the sides of her hips. I lowered my head, nuzzling the soft swell of skin, using my thumbs to flick her nipples. They hardened right through the fabric, and I sucked one into my mouth.

"You are beautiful," I whispered, lifting my gaze to hers.

"Thank you." Her hands roamed up my chest and onto my shoulders. "So are you."

I tugged the fabric of her bra down so her breasts popped over the cup. God, what a feast. They were round and the perfect size for my hands, with pale pink nipples that stood at attention, just waiting for me.

"Tell me what you like," I said.

"Everything. The harder the better."

"Rough and hard will come later. First, I will taste every inch of you." I moved my hand around to her back and undid the clasp of her bra before sliding it away from her body. She was in nothing but those tiny lace panties and I nearly lost my mind. She was thin but curvy, with a small waist and lush hips. Her skin was fair, with a faint golden hue that told me she probably got a tan in the summer from spending time outside. The landing strip of curls between her legs was golden as well, a few shades darker than the hair on her head.

As far as I was concerned, this gorgeous woman was sheer perfection, and I was luckier than I deserved to be.

I slid my hands down the outside of her thighs, reveling in how smooth her skin was. Hooking my fingers into the delicate bows on each side of her panties, I tugged them down and leaned closer to trail kisses along the inside of her thigh.

"Kon..." Her voice was a breathy whisper as her legs parted, making more room for me.

"I don't want to rush," I said, nuzzling the crease of her thigh. I slid a finger through her slick heat, and then bent my head to get my first taste. Her body shuddered lightly, so I licked her again, harder this time.

"Oh, god, yes." Her hips lifted, meeting my hungry mouth. When I nibbled her clit, she moaned loudly, the sound filled with need. I alternately sucked and licked, circling and teasing until she dug her fingers into my hair and pulled.

I held her firmly by the hips, keeping her pressed to the mattress as I devoured her. Her hips suddenly jerked and I felt her clench around me as a scream tore from her throat.

"Fuck, Kon, yes! Don't stop!"

I kept my mouth on her, continuing to kiss and touch her until her orgasm started to recede.

"Holy shit. That didn't take long." She sounded breathless and relaxed, which I loved.

I kissed my way up her stomach, pulling her close. "You are even more beautiful when you come."

"I think I just had my first real out-of-body experience." She giggled against my chest. "You know your way around a vagina, Mr. Volkov."

"Just wait," I said, giving her a playful smirk before reaching into my nightstand to grab a condom.

I slid off my boxers and straddled her as I rolled the condom down my aching erection.

Her eyes widened and she shook her head. "I should have known."

I arched a brow. "What?"

"That you'd be huge." She reached out, gently cupping my balls and running her knuckles along the side of my shaft. "That's going to feel so good inside of me."

"I think so, too." I leaned down to kiss her, slowing myself down enough to enjoy this moment.

I'd never given much thought to the first time I made love to a woman. With Svetlana, it had been a lifetime ago. With all the others, sex had been nothing but brief interludes of physical ecstasy that had nothing to do with the person I was with.

With Lucy, it was totally different, and I didn't know why.

I couldn't be bothered to worry about it, though. Not right now anyway.

Her fingers made their way into my hair again as we kissed and she spread her legs, inviting me in. I wanted to wait but when she arched her hips up, there was no way to hold out. I slowly pressed inside of her, inch by inch, until there was no more space between us. We were as close as two people could possibly be, our bodies completely in sync. Her beautiful blue eyes were glassy as our lips drifted together, barely touching.

"Fuckkk." She drew out the word as she squirmed beneath me.

"Too much?" I asked, stroking my hand over the side of her face.

"Nooo. *More*. Fuck me, Konstantin."

She didn't have to ask me twice.

CHAPTER SEVENTEEN

Lucy

MARIA LAUGHED as she walked past me near the entrance to Morelli Brothers.

"You've got a glow, Lucy. Is it Mr. Italian Beef?"

I smiled, putting my phone back in my pocket. I'd stopped outside the bakery entrance when I got a text from Konstantin and replied to it. Now I was waiting for a response.

"It is," I admitted. "Not that I'm not a modern woman who can't glow without a man, but this time…yeah."

"How was your Thanksgiving?" she asked me.

The glow she'd noticed was from my night with Kon, but the day had also been great. Sawyer's house had been full of his teammates and their families, and I'd been part of the group. I'd been reminded that Sawyer wasn't alone here. When the time came for me to leave, his teammates would still have his back.

"It was fantastic. Probably the best I've ever had. How was yours?"

She sighed. "Loud. But good. I love my family, even when they drive me crazy." She reached for the handle to the bakery's front door, but then paused. "Don't tell my dad and uncle I was smoking. They think I quit."

"Your secret is safe with me."

I hadn't even noticed her smoking because I'd been so immersed in my phone. Kon's text had given me butterflies, and his next one did, too.

Kon: Yes. I can be there around 4.

I'd invited him over to help Sawyer and me eat leftovers from yesterday and then watch hockey. The fridge was overflowing. And even though we had leftover pie for days, I'd come to the bakery to get the brownies I was hooked on.

Lucy: See you then. And feel free to get handsy under the blanket during the movie.

Kon: I won't be able to help myself.

The butterflies returned as I slipped my phone into my coat pocket. I'd only taken one step toward the bakery door when I was whipped backward by a powerful arm around my waist.

For a second, I was too stunned to react. But then I kicked and clawed as hard as I could, terror sending bile rising up my throat.

My feet didn't find anything but air, but my nails sank into the flesh of the hand holding me, and the one clamped over my mouth. I writhed against the powerful hold as I was carried toward the alley next to the bakery.

I couldn't let myself be taken into that alley. I could be raped or murdered and no one would even see it going down. Using both of my hands, I was able to get one of the man's fingers between my teeth, and I bit down hard with every ounce of strength I had.

"Christ." His growl became a cry of pain as I sank my teeth deeper, tasting the tang of his blood.

I'd break my teeth if I had to. I was going to fight him as hard as I could.

He dragged me closer to the alley, moving his hand from my mouth.

"Where is it, you bitch?" he asked, his voice gruff. "He knows you took copies of everything."

I wasn't surprised that Nate had sent this guy. How far was he willing to go to save himself?

It was hard to take a full breath with his arm

clamped around me, but I screamed as loudly as I could, hooking a foot around the corner of the building and trying to keep him from getting me into the alley.

"Hey!" An older woman walking a dog had seen us from the other side of the street. "Get your hands off her!"

She ran across the street as my assailant pulled me around the corner of the building, my shoe falling to the ground. He shoved me against the brick wall so hard my teeth shook, then clamped his hand back over my mouth.

"Where the fuck is it?"

He was so close my stomach rolled. I closed my eyes and drove my knee up into his balls, but he closed his legs before I made it all the way.

When he took his hand from my mouth, I was about to scream when he landed a punch to my face that knocked the breath out of me. Pain radiated through my cheek and I whimpered, trying not to panic but failing.

"That's a pretty face you got there," he said. "I'd hate to have to break your nose, but I will."

I tried to dart out from his hold, but he slammed me against the wall again. I cringed, waiting for the next blow to land.

There was a loud thudding sound, but nothing hurt. His hold on me loosened.

"Get the fuck off of her," a male voice said.

A long stick was jabbed into my attacker's stomach from the side, and I was finally free of his hold. My hand flew up to my injured face and I saw Luigi aiming the handle of a push broom at my attacker, Maria standing beside him wielding a snow shovel.

She'd hit him over the head with it.

"Get out of here, punk," Luigi said, pointing the broomstick at the man.

My attacker grabbed the broomstick and pushed it aside, then shoved Luigi against the wall. Maria swung the shovel at his head again, landing a hard blow. He turned to her with a murderous glare and I did the only thing I could think of—I barreled into him at full force.

It didn't help much. He shoved me to the ground and turned back to Maria.

"You like to fight girls and old men, you pussy?" a male voice said.

Mario stood at the entrance to the alleyway, a knife in hand. His expression was grim and determined.

"Girls, get inside the bakery," he said. "The cops are on their way."

Maria moved immediately, but I stayed frozen in place. I couldn't leave and risk my attacker getting that knife and turning it on Mario.

"Lucy, come on," Maria urged. "We have to go."

Luigi got to his feet, limping as he went to stand beside his brother.

Maria tugged on my arm, passing Luigi the shovel.

"Go," Luigi urged me.

I let Maria pull me into the bakery door, where I immediately ran behind the counter, searching every surface.

"Where are the knives?" I demanded.

"We aren't going back out there," Maria said. "The cops are on their way.

"We can't just leave them."

She steered me toward the back of the bakery. "Uncle Mario was Special Ops in the Army back in the day. He knows how to handle himself."

I wanted to believe her, but Mario and Luigi were bakers, not mercenaries. What if this was it? What if that vile criminal outside got the knife, killed both Mario and Luigi, and then came in here for me?

I grabbed my phone from my coat pocket and sent a hurried text to Sawyer.

Lucy: There's a manilla envelope hidden beneath the

dresser in your guest room. If something happens to me, you have to get it to the person it's addressed to. Don't tell anyone about it. Just deliver it.

I hit send, and a couple of seconds later, the door of the bakery opened and Mario walked in panting. Luigi was right behind him. Luigi locked the door once they were both inside.

"He took off," Mario said, sounding defeated. "He was too fast for these old dogs."

"You guys saved me," I said, my voice breaking with emotion. "I don't know how to thank you enough for what you did."

Luigi was carrying my bag, which I'd apparently left behind on the sidewalk. "Weird that the guy didn't even take this," he said. "He must have forgotten it."

They thought I'd been the victim of a random mugging. I didn't correct them.

"Dad, you need to sit down," Maria said. "I'll get ice for your knee."

He waved a hand. "I'll be fine. I just tweaked something when that asshole pushed me."

"Get Lucy some ice, too," Mario said.

He put the knife down on the counter and then put an arm around his brother to support him.

"You're going to the office to sit down," he said.

Luigi didn't argue this time. He and I were both

sitting in the back office when the police arrived. They were questioning me when my brother showed up, his eyes wide and panicked.

"What happened?" he asked me, taking in my face.

"I was attacked out front."

His eyes widened. "What, like *mugged*? Jesus, I pinged your phone as soon as I got your text. Why didn't you wake me up and ask me to drive you here?"

I looked at my lap, then turned back to him.

"I'll tell you everything once I finish this police interview. I'm okay, Sawyer. The owners of this place saved me. Mario, Luigi, and Maria."

He furrowed his brow, probably at the mention of Mario and Luigi. I'd have to explain later.

"Hi there, I'm Maria Morelli."

Maria passed my brother a cup of coffee, her eyes alight as she looked at him.

"Thank you," he said. "I mean, for the coffee, but mostly for what you did for my sister."

"Ma'am, have you reported any of this to the police back in Spokane?" the officer questioning me asked.

"No, because...I couldn't."

The officer's expression was a cross between sympathy and aggravation.

"It sounds like this guy could be behind bars by tonight if you'd just tell me everything you know. We need more to go on than a pissed-off ex who may or may not have sent someone to threaten you."

I wanted to tell him everything, but I couldn't. Nate had made sure of that.

"If I remember anything else, I'll reach out to you," I said.

"Was he threatening or abusive when you were together?"

Reluctantly, I shook my head.

"Ma'am, it's important that you're honest with me," the officer said.

"Look, she answered your questions," Sawyer said. "If anything else comes up, we'll reach out."

"Officer, how about some cinnamon rolls and coffee?" Maria offered. "Just a tiny little thank you. We're so grateful for your bravery and service."

His expression softened. Apparently, Maria knew how to butter up more than just rolls.

"That would be appreciated," he said, passing me a business card. "If you need anything else, you can reach me here, and it rings to the front desk twenty-four hours if I'm not in."

Maria took his arm. "You probably hardly get any breaks at all. Serving and protecting is such hard work. I'm going to send you along with a whole tray of cinnamon rolls."

"Lucy, what the hell?" Sawyer said, running a hand through his hair.

I gave him a look, letting him know we weren't discussing this here.

"I need to text Kon, and then can you follow me back home?" I asked.

"Yeah, of course."

I took out my phone, trying to decide how to phrase this. Kon was going to lose his shit, no matter how I described what had just gone down.

"I'm going to go introduce myself to, uh…Mario and Luigi," Sawyer said, gesturing. "I'll meet you up front when you're ready."

"Okay."

I typed out a message to Kon, deleted it, and then typed out another. Vagueness was probably best until we could talk face-to-face.

Lucy: Something happened this morning. I'm okay. I'll tell you about it when you come over later.

CHAPTER EIGHTEEN

Kon

TERRIFIED DIDN'T COME CLOSE to what I felt when I saw the bruises on Lucy's beautiful face and neck. Some motherfucker had put his hands on my woman—I didn't give a shit how we defined our relationship at the moment but she was mine—and whoever it was had to pay.

"I'm fine," she said for what had to be the hundredth time.

"You are *not* fine," I growled. It was impossible to hide my annoyance as I glanced at Sawyer. "How did you let her move in with this creep?"

Sawyer glared back at me. "*Dude.* She's a grown-ass woman. She said she loved him. When I met him,

I thought he was kind of boring, but she seemed happy." He paused, turning to his sister. "But you weren't, were you? By the time you met Nate, Annie was sick. So you weren't going to tell me anything like that."

Lucy sighed. "I wasn't *unhappy*. I just wasn't *happy* happy. Like you and Annie. But I thought maybe that kind of love wasn't in the cards for me. It's not like our parents had a relationship like that, or any of my friends, for that matter."

Sawyer's face tightened but he merely nodded. "I wish you'd talked to me, sis."

"Things were fine. Until they weren't."

"You cannot live this way," I protested. "Afraid they will come after you every time you leave the house. I want you to come to my place for a while."

"Fuck that!" Sawyer snapped. "I can protect her."

"I never said you couldn't, but they know where you live. They don't know anything about me." I met his gaze, all but daring him to contradict me.

"I have a plan," Lucy said, getting up and grabbing her laptop from the counter. "Look at this." She opened it and brought up a screen showing an old, dilapidated building that looked very European.

"What is this?" I asked.

"It's a villa in a town in Italy called Chevalia. It's about thirty minutes south of Tuscany." She seemed excited as she scrolled through the pictures. "The town is struggling, losing population because it's hard to find work and tourists don't find their way there too often. They're offering foreigners homes and apartments for dirt cheap—like less than a thousand Euro—with the only stipulations being that you renovate the place within three years and live there for five." Her smiled was broad, her eyes filled with excitement. "I've been in touch with an international school in Europe looking for English teachers to do tutoring online for students trying to improve their English, so I've potentially got a job lined up. They'll never find me there and I can start over."

Something sour twisted in my gut, but I didn't dare say anything because she looked so damn excited. Hell, if I wasn't a professional athlete making nearly seven million dollars a year, I'd probably be interested in going with her. But I couldn't. I also didn't think her starting over in a foreign country so far away from me was going to work now that we'd found each other.

Except maybe she didn't feel the same way I did, which kind of sucked.

"You can't move to Italy!" Sawyer finally said what I'd been thinking, eyes just like his sister's narrowing angrily. "You're all I have, Luce. And I refuse to let him chase you, not just out of Spokane and away from your job, but out of the fucking country."

"But I want to," she said softly. "It'll be an adventure. I've always wanted to travel, I have money saved up to renovate the villa, and maybe I can turn it into a bed-and-breakfast or something. Then you can come spend the off-season with me."

"Absolutely not." Sawyer folded his arms across his chest. "I won't allow it."

Lucy's eyes narrowed, a dangerous glint in them I'd never seen before. "Last I checked, you aren't my father and—as you pointed out—I am a grown woman. I don't need your permission."

"Goddamn, Lucy!" Sawyer started to yell but I put a hand on his arm.

"Wait," I said, trying to wrap my head around being the voice of reason. "The conversation about Italy is separate. But the more immediate situation is Lucy's safety. Nate cannot be allowed to just terrorize you. And you do not know for sure he won't find you in Italy if he has friends in law enforcement. Then what?"

Lucy scowled. "I'm just exploring my options and figuring things out. If Europe doesn't work out, there are tons of sleepy little towns all over the US where I could disappear for a while."

I felt like I was missing something about this

story, but Lucy had been attacked today and Sawyer was already in a foul mood, so I didn't want to dig any deeper right now. However, I was going to press the subject of her coming home with me, whether Sawyer liked it or not.

"That must be Boone," Lucy said when the doorbell rang. She'd invited him at the last minute since there was so much food leftover and Boone loved to eat. She got up to answer the door and I wasn't surprised when Sawyer grabbed my forearm as I tried to follow.

"What the fuck are you doing with my sister?" he asked.

"Dating," I replied, forcing myself not to react to the way he was holding my arm. I didn't like to be manhandled and he was one of the few people who could get away with it. For a short time, anyway.

"I told you she was off-limits."

"She is not a child and we do not need your permission." I was willing to let a lot slide when it came to Sawyer, but not my relationship with Lucy. It hadn't been long, but she was already too important to me.

"This is a huge betrayal."

"I have betrayed nothing," I said, yanking my arm free. "I care about her. I like her. I will never let anything happen to her. I will treat her a thousand times better than that fucker who's trying to hurt her."

Sawyer sighed, shaking his head. "I know that. I'm sorry. But I don't want…" He lifted his hands. "I know how we think. How we *are*. Professional athletes. Until we find the right one, the woman that's going to be our forever, we're dogs. Look at Rory. I don't fucking want that for her."

"I am not like that. When I am with a woman, that's it." I made a slashing motion with my hand. "Unless and until it doesn't work out, I will be good to her. Faithful. Kind. Whatever she needs. You have my word."

"Does she like you enough to not move to Italy or Bumfuck wherever?"

Now I was the one who sighed. "It is too soon for this conversation."

"That's what I was afraid of."

It was a fun evening hanging out with Sawyer, Lucy, and Boone, despite the faint tension in the air. Sawyer was annoyed about our relationship but resigned to it, Lucy seemed on edge about everything, and I was trying to walk the line between supportive and protective. The two were hard to mesh sometimes.

"So get this," Boone said when the movie we'd watched, *Avengers: Age of Ultron*, ended. "I heard from Missy yesterday."

We all turned to stare at him.

"She said she wants to talk."

"Please tell me you said no," Lucy whispered, her eyes wide. She'd become very protective of Boone since Missy had dumped him, and it was cute seeing her taking on the role of big sister.

"Well." He cleared his throat. "Kind of?"

Sawyer groaned. "Come on, man. She couldn't have been that good in bed."

Boone punched his arm. "It's not that. But I feel like if I loved her enough to ask her to marry me, we deserve at least a conversation. I told her I'd think about it since we're leaving on a road trip Sunday, which gives me a little time to figure out what I want to say."

I shook my head. "You are stupid."

Boone chuckled. "I'm trying to make sure I'm over her. I think I am. In fact, I'm almost positive, but again—I asked her to spend her life with me. That has to mean something. If I don't at least listen to what she has to say, what does that say about the man I am? It's not like she cheated or stole from me.

She said some unkind things, but those are just words. I'm man enough to understand when someone speaks without thinking." He held up a hand as all three of us started to talk at once. "I'm serious, guys. I've got this. I have no plans to get back with her. I just think we need to clear the air."

"I'm going to kick your ass if you sleep with her," Lucy muttered. "Not even kidding."

"On that note, I think I need to get home," Boone said, getting up. "We have a morning skate and a game tomorrow night. You guys should come." He looked at Sawyer. "Yeah, I'm talking to you, dickhead."

Sawyer scowled. "Maybe. I'll think about it."

"I want to go," Lucy said. "I haven't been to a game since I got here."

"I will arrange for you to sit in the owners' box," I said automatically. "You cannot wander the arena alone. Not with those men after you."

She nodded slowly. "Okay."

"Now get your things. You're coming to my place until Sunday." I hated going all bossy caveman on her, but her safety was nonnegotiable. If she wanted to argue, I was ready.

Sawyer looked ready to protest but Lucy gave him a pointed look. "You mind your business." She turned back to me. "And I would appreciate if you *asked* me to come over, instead of ordering me around."

I reached for her, pulling her against me. "I am worried about you, Lucy. Will you please stay with me for a couple of days so I know you're safe?"

She smiled, shaking her head. "Much better. And yes, I will. Thank you."

It only took her a few minutes to pack a small overnight bag, grab a few of those brownies she loved, and then we were on our way. Sawyer hadn't said much, Boone left before we did, and the ride to my condo was quiet.

"You are okay?" I asked softly.

"I'm frustrated," she admitted. "I hate that my situation is blowing back on people I care about. Sawyer. The Morellis. You and Boone."

"It is not a problem for me," I said, taking her hand. "I want you with me, Lucy. Even if this wasn't going on, I liked having you spend the night last time. I would like you to spend many more nights with me."

"Kon, you know I'm leaving, right? Probably not until after the holidays, but then..." Her voice trailed off and she looked away.

"And what if I handle this situation with Nate?"

"I don't want you getting hurt."

I snorted. "Sweetheart, you have no idea who I

used to be. I promise you—it would be very difficult for him to hurt me."

"Now that's the most mysterious thing you've ever said," she responded, curiosity in her voice. "Who did you used to be?"

"It is a very long story for another time." I'd just pulled into my parking space and was grabbing her overnight bag out of the back seat. "But do not worry about my safety. I can take care of myself."

She made a face but didn't press it since a couple of my neighbors were waiting at the elevators, evidently feeling chatty. We made small talk on the way up to my floor and then I let her walk inside the condo ahead of me after I unlocked my front door.

"I've done nothing but eat the last week," she said, kicking off her boots. "I think I need a workout."

I slapped her ass. "I can think of many ways to work you out. Sex burns calories, you know."

"Oh, really?" She turned, laughing as I flipped on the lights.

"Konstantin." A soft voice spoke from the living room and I immediately yanked Lucy behind me.

Then I recognized the voice.

What in the ever-loving fuck was Svetlana doing here?

CHAPTER NINETEEN

Lucy

Svetlana's eyes widened as she took me in. Then they narrowed.

"How did you get in here?" Kon demanded. "You gave the key back when we broke up."

She shrugged and said something to him in Russian. He rolled his eyes and blew out a breath.

"I should go," I said, giving him a tight smile.

"No," he said firmly. "*She* will go."

His ex's gaze was back on me, disdain in her tone as she gave Kon an earful in Russian. Despite the situation, I felt for her. Her face was gaunt and her dirty blond hair was *actually* dirty. The beat-up coat she wore looked more like roadkill than a fur.

Kon responded to her in Russian, the tone of his voice rising with every word. I wasn't mad at him—clearly he hadn't planned this, but I also didn't want to stay and continue being insulted in a foreign language.

Svetlana stood and walked over to us. I backed up a couple of steps because I'd already been punched in the face once today, and that was enough.

Kon took out his wallet and passed Svetlana several hundred-dollar bills. My stomach rolled as he held the money out and she protested, gesturing around the apartment. She took off her coat and tossed it on a chair.

This didn't feel like a conversation between two people who were over. He clearly wanted her to leave, and was willing to pay for it, but what if I hadn't been here with him?

"No," he said firmly, offering her the cash again.

She scowled at me, and Kon said something to her in Russian. I didn't want to be here. Taking my phone from my bag, I texted Sawyer.

Lucy: Can you please come pick me up at Kon's ASAP?

Sawyer: Yep, on my way. What's up?

Lucy: His ex is here.

Sawyer: Yikes, she's a disaster. I'll pick you up out front.

Kon and Svetlana were still engaged in an animated conversation when I opened the door to leave.

"Lucy, no," he said, giving me an imploring look. "This is not what it looks like. She's in trouble with a pimp."

"I'm going back to Sawyer's," I said. "You guys need to work this out without me here."

He shook his head, putting his hands on his hips. "Please don't go. I'm trying to get her to take this money and go."

"She wants to stay here, doesn't she?" I asked him, knowing the answer.

"It does not matter that she wants to. She is not staying here. I have not been with her since we broke up. I swear it. She just has nowhere else to turn for help."

Svetlana stuck out a hip, arms crossed as she addressed him in their native language again. I grabbed my bag, opened the door, and walked out of the apartment. I'd only made it a few steps when Kon caught up to me.

"I didn't ask her to come here," he said pleadingly. "I have nothing to do with her anymore. Please don't go, Lucy. You are the only one I want here."

I smiled sadly. "Look, I'm not mad at you. This is

just awkward as hell. Sawyer's on his way to pick me up."

His gaze darkened. "She is...I do not know the word in English. She would like for you to leave because she does not want me to be happy. I will never be with her again. I promise. But I cannot..." He exhaled hard. "She saved my life back in Russia, Lucy. I want to tell you about it but I need you to stay so I can."

Svetlana's voice sounded from the doorway of his apartment and we both turned. She was leaning against the doorframe, now wearing one of Kon's T-shirts and looking right at home.

I laughed bitterly. "Yeah, I'm out of here. And I am a little bit mad at you now."

"Fucking hell," he muttered. "I am sorry, Lucy. Let me wait for Sawyer with you. I don't want you out there alone."

I waved a hand, already heading toward the elevator. "By the time you got back in here, she'd be naked in your bed. I'm out."

"Don't go."

He continued following me, so I took the stairs instead of waiting for the elevator. I liked Kon, but drama was a deal breaker for me. After what happened this morning, I needed peace. Hot sex would have been a great bonus, but peace was paramount.

Icy wind whipped my hair into my face as I stood in front of his building. Part of me knew how Kon must be feeling right now. Svetlana looked like she wasn't getting enough to eat. I wasn't savage enough to send someone onto the streets cold and hungry. Cruel as it was, she wasn't exactly a top-tier prostitute, and it sickened me to think of any woman performing sex acts for a few bucks because it was the only way she could eat.

"Lucy, please."

Kon put his coat around my shoulders. It smelled faintly of leather and his cologne. The sweetness of the gesture tugged on my heartstrings.

"Take care of your shit," I said gently. "We'll talk later."

"If you stay, she will go."

I sighed heavily. "So, since I'm going, she's staying?"

He pushed his brows together, looking aggravated. "She is not here legally. If I call the police…"

"Maybe a free ticket home wouldn't be bad," I said gently. "She's in a bad situation here."

"And a worse one there. She would be dead within a few hours."

Sawyer pulled up and I gave Kon a sympathetic

look. "I trust you. I just...don't have the headspace for this right now. It's been a hell of a day."

He nodded, looking resigned. "I understand."

Sliding his coat from my shoulders, I passed it back to him and walked toward Sawyer's car.

"I'll talk to you later," I said.

He nodded again, his expression somber. I got in Sawyer's car and closed my eyes, eager to be anywhere but here.

"CROSS-CHECK," Sawyer muttered. "But of course, no call, because Cruse is the darling of every ref in this league."

We were in the first row at the Mavericks game, nothing but the glass separating us from the action. Sawyer refused to watch the game from a suite, because he wanted to be close to the action. It was my preference, too. Anytime he got our mom and me tickets to a game, they were close to the action.

Kon stretched during a break in the game. I'd never paid much attention to a goalie before now, and it was a harder job than I'd realized. Every time the puck was near his net, I was on the edge of my seat. His blocks were timed perfectly. One puck had slid past him and he'd yelled something in Russian that, from the sound of it, was one-hundred-percent profanity.

The Mavs were up 3–1, though. And the guys had all acknowledged Sawyer. This was his first game since Annie's death. No matter which side of the glass he was on, it was progress.

"You hungry?" Sawyer asked me.

I shook my head. "We can eat after this. Don't go back to the concession stand or you'll never make it back."

We'd gotten in line for slushies before the game started, and within a few seconds, the first fan recognized Sawyer. An actual mob had formed. People were pushing and yelling, trying to get autographs and photos. I'd held on to Sawyer's arm, my heart pounding in fear of someone getting hurt, when security guards had come and helped us get out. An usher had delivered our slushies.

"I can have stuff brought here," he said. "You want anything?"

"I wouldn't say no to some popcorn and a bottle of water."

He nodded and typed out a text on his phone.

After we got home from Kon's last night, I'd gone straight to bed and slept for twelve hours straight. I felt better, though my face still hurt and I didn't have much of an appetite.

It had taken a lot of makeup to cover the bruise on my face, and there was nothing I could do about the swelling. I was wearing a Mavericks hat pulled low, hoping to conceal my face as much as possible.

Sawyer leaned closer to me and said, "I vote we go out for dinner after the game. We have a lot to talk about."

I cringed inwardly because he was right. This morning, I'd told him I wasn't up for talking. Not only did he want to know what my text about the manilla envelope beneath my dresser meant, he wanted to tell me about Svetlana.

Though I'd hear him out, Svetlana was not someone I wanted to talk about. Kon had texted me this morning to ask when he could see me, and I still hadn't responded. I'd felt his gaze on me as he skated toward the goal earlier, and I liked it.

I liked *him*. A lot. And since I wasn't planning to stay here long term, I shouldn't have cared about his down-on-her-luck ex showing up and asking for his help.

I cared, though. Seeing her in his T-shirt had brought on a wave of jealousy like nothing I'd felt before. She was sending me a message: *I have a history with him, and you don't.*

"Where do you want to go for dinner?" I asked Sawyer.

He was out of the house, living life again. So whether I felt like talking or not, I would. We'd go out for dinner and discuss things because that's what adults did. I couldn't very well tell my brother to stop hiding behind booze and face up to his shit if I wasn't willing to face up to my own.

"There's an Italian place the team likes to go after games sometimes," he said. "But I don't know. We won't be able to talk if there are other people there."

"We can talk on the way there," I offered.

His expression turned serious. "You need to tell me everything, Luce. I can't help you if I don't know what we're up against."

"I'm not sure you can help at all," I said softly. "But I'll tell you everything anyway."

"Excuse me, Mr. Cain?" a child's voice called out.

Sawyer and I turned to see two young boys in Mavericks jerseys standing in the aisle.

"May we have your autograph?" one of them asked Sawyer.

They were so cute, both of them looking hope-fully at my brother. He looked slightly taken aback, but I didn't understand why.

"You guys know I'm not on the team anymore, right?" he said.

"You'll be back," the blond boy said.

The other boy turned around and showed

Sawyer the back of his jersey, which had Sawyer's name and number on it.

"You're my favorite player," he said. "I don't let my mom wash this when you guys are on a winning streak. She says it gets smelly, but I don't care."

I swallowed hard, forcing myself not to get teary-eyed. This was what Sawyer needed—to know he was still wanted and needed on his team.

"Of course you can get autographs," he said, taking out his phone. "Let me reach out to someone really quick and see if we can get you some game pucks."

The boys exchanged an excited glance. Sawyer took pictures with them and signed some merchandise an usher brought down to our seats.

"When are you coming back?" one of the boys asked him. "We need you kicking ass out there."

"James, language," his mother scolded from nearby.

Sawyer grinned at her.

"I'm not sure," he said to the boy. "Soon, I hope."

I hoped with everything in me that he meant it.

Kon

DESPITE GETTING a win on the ice tonight, I was in a piss-poor mood when I got home from the arena. It had been twenty-four hours since Lucy had left my apartment and she still hadn't responded to any of my calls or texts. She'd been at the game tonight—I'd seen her through the glass—but she and Sawyer had left without coming back to the family lounge. So instead of spending my last night before a road trip with the woman I was falling for, I was going to spend it fighting with my ex.

Svetlana had no intention of leaving unless I forcibly removed her, and while I didn't want things to get ugly, I had no intention of letting her stay here. She'd already put me through enough. Our past was one thing, but my future was another.

I didn't acknowledge her as I went into my room to change out of my suit. I'd held out hope that she might be gone by the time I got back from the game, but it looked like she was trying to settle in and that wasn't happening.

When I walked back out to the living room, she was wrapped in a blanket with a bowl of popcorn on her lap. She held it out.

"Want some?" She spoke in Russian, a subtle reminder of one of our only remaining bonds, which irritated me even more.

"No." I put my hands on my hips and stared down at her. "What are you doing, Svetlana? You know you're not welcome here."

She sighed dramatically. "I don't have anywhere else to go. I can't go back to Russia, and my visa here in the US has run out. I can't legally get a job, so what do you expect me to do?"

"You should have thought of that before you cheated on me."

"We were going through a rough time," she said quietly, reaching out to grab the remote and lower the volume. "You were so busy trying to prove your-self on the team once we got to St. Louis, you had no time for me. We lost each other for a while, but now that we've had time apart—"

"I realize that I never loved you at all," I said flatly.

Her face crumpled a little, and I felt bad, but she had to take responsibility for her own actions.

"I was never *in love* with you," I clarified, since that was the truth and my intention was to be firm, not cruel. "You'll always be my friend, and I want to help, but you did this to yourself. I gave you everything you asked for. We got out of Russia, you didn't have to work, I made more money than either of us ever dreamed of, and you had a nice, uncomplicated life. Then—"

"You're the one who wanted us to fit in!" she snapped, interrupting me. "You're the one who wanted me to learn English and make friends with your teammates and act like the others."

"I wanted you to make friends with my teammates' *wives*," I said, clenching my jaw. "Not my teammates."

"Keegan paid attention to me," she spat. "He liked me. We had fun together. All you ever wanted to do was stay home, learn English, and watch TV. Keegan liked to go out dancing and to fancy dinners. We went to concerts and parties. I never got to have fun like that in Russia and you wouldn't do it once we came here. Was it so wrong for me to want to live a little?"

"And now?" I asked, meeting her gaze. "How much fun are you having now, living on the street and doing who knows what to feed yourself?"

"I'm sorry, okay? I screwed up, but you owe me."

There it was.

The guilt.

The reminder of what she'd done for me.

I rubbed my hands down over my face.

"Listen to me." I sat across from her on the couch. "I'll never forget what you did, but I paid you back for that by getting you out of there and giving you the life that we had started to build here. *You* chose to walk away. You chose another man. You can't blame me for moving on."

"They'll kill me if I go back," she whispered.

"Then go somewhere else. You have family in Tashkent, yes? I'll give you money to get started over there. An apartment. A job. Whatever you need to get settled."

"But they barely know me," she whispered, tears puddling in her eyes. "And I don't know them. I haven't seen them since I was a child."

"You can't legally stay or work in the US and you can't go back to Russia. Uzbekistan is an easy, safe choice for you. Reach out to your family. Your aunt always loved you. I'm sure that hasn't changed."

She didn't say anything for a long time, angrily swiping at her eyes before looking at me again.

"The American girl—does she know who you are? And what you're capable of? That your fists were literally declared lethal weapons by the police in Siberia?"

I sighed. "That was a long time ago. It's not who I am anymore."

"Leopards do not change their spots. Someday, she'll see the beast beneath the calm exterior and won't know how to deal with you. And she'll leave you too. What then?"

"What I do and who I do it with is none of your business now." I slowly got to my feet. "So go get your shit. You're going to a hotel."

She scowled. "I don't want to go to a hotel."

"Well, you can go to a hotel that I pay for, or you can sleep on the street, but you're not staying here. You choose."

She huffed out a breath. "Listen, I didn't want things to go this way. I got pregnant but had a miscarriage. Keegan was furious and accused me of having an abortion. That's why he kicked me out. But I didn't. Why would I? Giving birth to a baby here in America was one way I could potentially stay. He didn't believe me. So when he threw me out, he kept almost all my things. I barely have any clothes, Konstantin. I have nothing. Can you call him to try to get some of my things back?"

"I'll give you money," I said quietly. There was zero chance I was going to talk to Keegan fucking Miller about anything. "I have an extra suitcase in the guest room you can take with you, and I'll pay for your hotel room until I get back from my trip. I'm going to tell the doorman you're not welcome here and I'm having the locks changed, so don't even think about coming back. Do you understand me?"

"Fine." She slowly got to her feet. "You're making a mistake, though. That pretty American is never going to understand you or know how to handle you when you lose control. And don't kid yourself, Konstantin. We both know, eventually, you're going to lose control."

———

It was a relief to finally drop Svetlana off at one of those extended-stay motels. I paid for two weeks in advance after stopping at Walmart and letting her buy some groceries, toiletries, and clothes. It was late by the time I got back to my apartment, but I reached out to Lucy right away anyway.

Kon: Hi, it's me again. Svetlana is gone. Please talk to me, Lucy. I miss you and would like to explain everything.

There was no response, and I drifted off to sleep with my phone on my chest, my dreams haunted by memories of the past. Fighting for my life, both literally and figuratively. Living in the slums of Siberia. Trying to balance hockey with staying alive. Using my fists so my grandmother and I didn't starve.

I woke with a start when my alarm went off, my neck stiff from tossing and turning all night. I didn't have time to feel sorry for myself, though. I had to pack and meet the team at the airport in three hours. Normally I packed the night before, but I'd obviously had to deal with Svetlana. Now I was running behind and still no word from Lucy, which was starting to piss me off.

None of what was going on had been my fault. I'd been there for her since she'd gotten to St. Louis, supporting both the situation with Sawyer and whatever was going on with her ex, which she still hadn't explained. I'd tried to be there for her in every way I could, never pushing her or asking for anything in return. Yet, the first time I could have used some emotional support, she wouldn't even let me explain what was going on.

Sometimes it felt like I had the worst luck when it came to women.

I'd reach out one more time and then I was done.

The ball would be in her court.

This time I called, though.

It rang four times, and I was sure it was going to voice mail when I was surprised to hear her voice on the line. "Good morning, Kon."

"Lucy. Hello. I didn't think you would answer."

"I know. I'm sorry. It's been a rough couple of days."

"Is Sawyer okay?"

"Believe it or not, he's doing better."

"I'm glad." I cleared my throat. "So, I do not have much time. I have to leave for the airport soon, but I wanted you to know that there is nothing between me and Svetlana. Not now, not ever again. She's gone and I'm changing the locks of my condo."

"Okay."

"The other night, you said you trusted me. Is this still true?"

Lucy hesitated but then said, "Yes, I do. You've never given me any reason not to. I was just tired and overwhelmed. Seeing your ex standing there in one of your shirts didn't help."

"I threw it away," I said quickly. "I would never wear it again after seeing her in it."

She chuckled. "Okay, I can live with that."

"When I come back, I want to see you, tell you everything, explain the past. This will help you to understand who I am. Maybe also help us get to know each other better."

"I'd like that." Her voice sounded softer now, like we were finally back on track. At least I hoped so.

"I hate to ask, but I need a favor."

"If I can."

"Can you and Sawyer come here to wait for the locksmith? I can ask the doorman, but I prefer someone who cannot be bribed. Could you do this for me so I know for sure Svetlana cannot get back in?"

"I...yes. We'll come and wait for them. Are they coming now?"

"They said in the next two hours."

"All right. We're just finishing breakfast. We can head over in a few."

"I will probably be gone, but I appreciate this. And I promise, when I get home, I'm going to make all of this up to you."

"You sure are," she said with a soft chuckle.

"I'll call you tonight from the hotel."

"Talk to you then."

I hung up and stared at the phone for a few seconds.

At least Lucy was talking to me again.

If only I could get Svetlana's words out of my head.

Someday, she'll see the beast beneath the calm exterior and won't know how to deal with you. And she'll leave you too.

CHAPTER TWENTY-ONE

Lucy

THE BACK of my neck prickled with awareness as I walked into the kitchen and heard someone breathing heavily. I ran to the knife block on the counter and pulled one out, my heart racing as I scanned the room.

"Who's there?" I demanded, backing up until I was against the counter.

I'd had a nightmare last night about being grabbed from behind and suffocated. The attack in the alley was never far from my mind—both consciously and unconsciously.

My gaze landed on the heavy breather. It was

Sawyer, who was curled up in a ball in the wide doorway to the dining room.

"Oh my god, are you okay?" I ran over to him and dropped to my knees.

He sprawled out on his back. "I just…ran five miles. I'm dying, Luce."

My shoulders slumped with relief and I put the knife down. "What the hell, Sawyer? You haven't exercised in like eight months. You need to start smaller."

He furrowed his brow. "What's with the knife?"

"I thought you might be a heavy-breathing murderer."

After a single note of laughter, he clutched his stomach. "Oh shit. I'm regretting the two hundred crunches I knocked out before my run."

"Let's get you off the floor."

He gave me a pathetic look. "Let me die here."

"You can't die today because I want to go shopping, and while I would love to go alone"

"You're not going out alone," he protested. "Are you out of your mind?"

I got up and went to the refrigerator, getting him a bottle of water. When I returned, I held the water in one hand and extended my other one to him to help him up.

He groaned as he got himself up, not bothering

to use my hand.

"I couldn't even play high school hockey in this condition," he grumbled. "I need to just retire and save my dignity."

I passed him the water. "Don't you think it's premature to decide that after one day of trying to get back in shape?"

"I'm not the same Sawyer Cain as before," he said after draining half the bottle. "That's what people would expect if I went back."

"One day at a time. Which reminds me...when are you going to start going to your AA meetings?"

We'd talked a lot after the game the other night. For two people who had been living together, there was a lot we needed to tell each other. One of the topics I'd broached was AA meetings, which he'd agreed were a good idea.

"I looked up the schedule. There's a Monday meeting at a church a couple of miles away."

I just looked at him in silence. He shifted on his feet and sighed heavily.

"So Monday," he finally said. "I'm going to start on Monday."

"Hey, you know what everyone who cares about you wants, right?"

He shrugged, still aggravated. "For me to go to meetings for the rest of my life?"

"For you to be healthy and happy," I said gently. "And as far as I'm concerned, you're well on your way. If you go back to hockey, great, but if you don't, that's great, too. You're part of the world again, and you're not muting your feelings with alcohol. That's all I wanted for you."

He nodded, then took off the hoodie he was wearing, revealing a sweat-soaked T-shirt.

"I get that, but I need a purpose," he said. "I can't just wake up and sit at home every day."

"You have enough money, though. You can coach hockey if you want to. Or travel. Hell, come travel with me if you want to."

He finished off the water. "I'm not ready to decide anything. I'm just trying to lose this fucking beer belly and get back to a place where I can run five miles without feeling like I'm about to die."

"Okay. Do you need to shower before we go shopping?"

He nodded. "Where are we going?"

"There are a few stores I want to go to, but they're all at the same mall."

He held up a finger in warning. "I'm not taking you to Victoria's Secret to buy lingerie to wear for Kon."

"That's fine. I'll take myself there if I want to go."

He shook his head, frowning. "You aren't taking

yourself anywhere. You could have been killed the other day."

"You can always track me with my phone, and I also ordered an AirTag in case you need to find me and I don't have my phone with me."

"So I'll know where your dead body is located?" he deadpanned. "Awesome, thanks."

I smiled, glad to see the old Sawyer was slowly reemerging. "No need to argue. I don't need to go to Victoria's Secret. I can buy my thongs at another store."

He groaned and covered his face with his hands. "Don't fucking tell me that, Luce. It's hard enough to imagine you with my teammate. I don't need any visuals."

"You thought everything was great when I was with Nate, but it turned into a living hell when I ran across that information at his office. Kon treats me better than any man ever has."

"Yeah, but he's just a distraction until you leave, right? He's my teammate, Luce, but you're my sister. If this is just a fling…" He cringed and put his hands up. "Then whatever. But it feels like it's more to you."

"Just go take a shower so we can go shopping, Dr. Laura. I didn't ask you for relationship advice."

He pointed a finger at me as he walked away. "I didn't use the word relationship. That was you."

I folded my arms, trying to come up with a witty comeback, but failing. I was living life one day at a time right now, too. But I couldn't do that forever. Things with Kon couldn't last, so I planned to enjoy every moment I could while I still had him.

———

THAT EVENING, I felt sexy as hell when I opened Sawyer's front door and Kon looked me up and down, mumbling something in Russian.

For the first time in my life, I'd gone for it. I'd bought black leather pants, black booties, and a red wrap shirt that showed off my cleavage. The pants weren't the shiny kind—I wasn't going for the dominatrix look—but they were actually very comfortable.

When Sawyer got a look at me in the outfit, he shook his head and went down to his office, grumbling that I should try not to "come home tomorrow carrying Kon junior."

"I am so lucky," Kon said, his gaze soft when it met mine. "You are...everything, Lucy. You are everything."

The butterflies in my stomach clamored. No man had ever thought I was everything. I was starting to realize that running across that damning information in Nate's office may have been the best thing that ever happened to me. That had brought me here.

"Are you ready to go?" I asked him.

"Yes, very much."

I put on my coat but skipped the hat because I'd spent too much time on my hair to ruin it. He took my hand as we walked to his car.

"We are trying a new restaurant," he said. "My agent got me the reservation. It's supposed to be the hottest ticket in St. Louis."

I smiled as he opened my car door. "Sounds like fun."

Once he was behind the wheel, he put his hand on my knee and looked me in the eye.

"You are the only woman I want, Lucy. Tell me you know you are the only one."

I nodded. "I do. I think most people have baggage."

He furrowed his brow, confused.

"Baggage means issues from past relationships," I explained.

"Ah." He put his hands on the wheel and started driving. "Well, my baggage is moving to Uzbekistan."

"Really?"

He nodded, looking relieved. "I hope she will do well, but I can't have her in my life anymore."

"Totally off topic, but I love your accent. You make the word 'Uzbekistan' sound sexy."

He grinned. "You want to hear some Russian dirty talk tonight?"

God, yes. The way he looked in that leather jacket, he could have pulled over and had me in the back seat right now, but I didn't let on.

"Maybe," I said coyly. "Let's see how the night goes."

He laughed, putting his hand on my thigh. "You are wet inside those sexy pants, and we both know it."

"I might be. And what about you? Are you feeling anything?"

He scoffed. "I have a third leg, but I plan to behave myself until later."

"You don't mind if I talk about it, though? Like if I told you I fantasized in the shower about riding you, that would be fine?"

He squeezed my thigh and groaned. "Absolutely fine. Wind me as tightly as you want, but just know that you may be sore tomorrow."

"I don't mind. I hope you don't just mean my pussy, though. I like it when you play rough with my nipples, too, and"

"Okay, no more," he said, cutting me off. "I won't make it all the way home if you don't stop."

I laughed lightly. "You said you liked it."

"I fucking love it, but wait until we finish dinner. Unless you want to get fucked up against a bathroom wall at this restaurant."

I considered the idea. "If I had a skirt on, I'd be in. That won't work with these pants, though."

The restaurant we went to was a renovated nightclub with tall ceilings and two levels. Techno music was playing low and there were colored light beams dancing on the walls.

"This place is weird," Kon declared when we sat down at our table.

"It's…unique," I agreed.

Our server told us the restaurant didn't have menus and that the chef would send out our meal one course at a time. I ordered a glass of wine and Kon ordered a beer as he eye-fucked my cleavage during our short wait for the first course.

"A cabbage dumpling?" Kon asked after the server had explained the tiny bundle in the middle of each plate.

"With a chile verde sauce," the server said proudly. "Enjoy."

Once we were alone, Kon met my gaze across the table.

"This is one bite of food," he said.

"Let's hope it's a good bite."

"I am starving." He shook his head and raised his hand to get our server's attention.

"Sir?" the server asked when she returned.

"Can I just get a hamburger?" Kon asked. "Or a pizza?"

The server knitted her brows together, her expression stunned.

"Um, there's braised beef in one of your other courses," she said. "We don't have menus; all we serve is the chef's selections."

He just looked at her for a couple of seconds, until I ended the moment that was quickly becoming awkward.

"Thanks, we'll just eat our dumplings."

The rest of the meal was similar; the server brought us a single bite of food on a plate and while most of the bites tasted good, by the time we ate our eighth bite—panna cotta—we were still hungry.

"Three hundred dollars for sixteen bites of food," Kon grumbled as he signed the check. "I'm sorry, Lucy. This wasn't what I expected."

"Want to get some takeout on the way to your place?" I asked.

"Very much. And as soon as we get home, I plan to get you out of those clothes."

I smiled, desire swirling in my belly. "I plan to let you."

CHAPTER TWENTY-TWO

Kon

WE PICKED up Chinese on the way home, and Lucy and I shared an egg roll during the drive. The restaurant had been upscale and classy, but definitely not a place for two people who liked to eat. And apparently the two of us did.

"Still hungry?" I asked, putting the bags of food down once we were inside.

"Mm-hmm." She tugged the lapels of my sport coat. "But food can wait."

"What would you like to do instead?" I asked, pretending not to know what she was talking about.

"I'd like to get up close and personal with your

tats," she murmured, working on the buttons of my dress shirt.

I smirked. "And I want to get up close and personal with your tits."

She squealed as I tossed her over my shoulder and carried her to the bedroom. I dumped her on the bed before shrugging out of my jacket and throwing my belt to the side. I watched as she pulled off the sexy red blouse she'd been wearing that had given me a fantastic view of her tits all night. I was almost sorry to see it come off, except having access to her breasts would be better than simply imagining them beneath the silky fabric.

I dipped my head, fastening my lips to hers as I cupped her breasts in my hands. She still tasted vaguely of the wine she'd had earlier, and I slid my mouth along the curve of her neck. Her head fell back and my gaze followed the long golden hair that tumbled around us. God, she was beautiful. How had I gotten so lucky to find a woman like Lucy?

"You make me so hard," I growled against her throat.

"You make me so wet," she panted.

Her eyes burned with arousal as she ran her hands down my torso. My shirt was still on, though mostly unbuttoned, and she hurriedly unfastened the remaining ones, finally pushing the fabric off my shoulders. She ran warm, wet lips across my collarbone, sliding them down to my nipples. When she grazed her teeth back and forth across one, my erection strained against my slacks and boxers.

"I need you inside me, Kon," she said.

"Then I need you naked," I said, reaching around to unhook her bra. Somewhere along the way she'd lost her shoes, so now all that was left were those incredible leather pants that hugged her gorgeous figure. I slid them down her hips slowly, my body practically combusting when I saw she wore no panties beneath.

"Look at how sexy you are," I breathed, sliding a finger between her folds and slowly pressing the tip inside of her. "And very, very wet."

"I've been thinking about this for days." Her breath hitched as I pushed my middle finger all the way in and curved it slightly. I moved in and out a few times before slowly pulling it free and sliding it into my mouth, licking it clean.

"You taste much better than dessert."

"I believe you promised me a ride earlier," she moaned, her eyes never leaving my mouth.

"Yes, I did."

I peeled her pants the rest of the way down and then took care of my own clothes before settling on my back. Holding my hands for support, she straddled my hips and guided herself over my cock. I handed her a condom and our eyes locked as she rolled it over my aching shaft.

"Such a big boy," she whispered, closing her eyes and sinking down all the way.

We both groaned as she bottomed out.

"God, that feels so fucking good," she said, rolling her hips back and forth, as if testing out what felt the best.

"Look at me when I'm inside of you," I said in a gruff voice. "Then fuck yourself on my cock."

Her blue eyes blinked open, her lips parted, and that glorious hair fell forward. Her perfect tits bounced as she moved up and down, and I couldn't do anything but go along for the ride because she was in control.

I loved the way she was setting the pace, taking what she wanted and giving me what I needed without even realizing it. It was like we'd been together much longer than we had, and I never wanted this to end. Her tight, wet heat had me fucking mesmerized, and as she picked up speed, there was nothing I could do but hold on and follow her lead.

"K-Konstantin!" Her voice was a cross between a pant and a moan, my name stuttering out of her just as her face contorted and my own world went white.

We crashed together, her pussy squeezing my cock like it belonged to her, and I held her down as I exploded inside of her.

It was loud and messy and absolutely fucking gorgeous.

Just like her.

"Beautiful Lucy." I reached up, pulling her down so the side of her face was on my chest. "That was incredible."

"I thought so too." She sighed, the long, lazy sound of a very satisfied woman.

And fuck if it didn't get me hard all over again knowing I'd done that to her.

We laid lay there for a long time, our bodies wound together, my hands slowly trailing over her skin. I wanted to get up, dispose of the condom, clean up a little so we could be more comfortable, but I didn't want to move. She felt magnificent, my cock still at half-mast and tucked inside her warm heat. Her hair tickled my arms and she kept pressing light kisses on my chest.

"How can you still be hard?" she murmured after about fifteen minutes.

"I'm not *still* hard," I explained with a laugh. "I'm hard *again*."

"What are you, seventeen?" she teased.

"I warned you tomorrow you would be sore."

"I'm looking forward to it." She nestled deeper against me. "I've never met anyone like you, Kon."

"And I have never met anyone like you." I gently grabbed a fistful of her hair and tugged just hard enough to force her to look at me. "This is why I don't want you to leave."

"What?" She seemed confused.

"I don't want you to go anywhere. To Europe or wherever you feel you have to hide from Nate. I like you. More than I have liked anyone in a long time. This is why I'd like to explain about Svetlana. My past. So you understand who I am and where I come from. And then maybe we can talk about us."

She didn't answer right away but slowly pulled away. "Okay, but first I have to pee," she said. "Then we can talk."

"Deal." I followed her into the bathroom and we cleaned up together before getting back into bed. She moved into my arms easily, reminding me again how good it was between us. That was why I had to tell her everything. Before we got any more involved.

"I grew up in Siberia," I told her quietly. "Very cold, very poor, very hard life."

"In my head I didn't think regular people lived there," she said. "I always thought of it as where a prison is."

"Yes. But regular people live there as well. When I was thirteen, my grandmother took me to another town, where there was work for her in a bakery and I could play hockey. I went to school in the morning and then to practice after, while my grandmother worked fourteen-hour days for us to live. This was when I met Svetlana. Her mother was dead and her father abused her both physically and sexually. At night, after my grandmother was asleep, I would help her sneak out and we would meet with our friends to drink, smoke, whatever trouble we could find."

"Sad, lonely teenagers with no one looking out for them," she said softly.

"Yes." I nodded, rubbing one of my hands up and down her arm as I talked. "It was okay for a while, but my grandmother fell. She broke her leg and there was no money for care, physical therapy, nothing. One of my friends, he told me about a place I could go to make money. Fighting."

"Like boxing?" she asked.

"More like MMA. Except without rules. Without referees. Two men in a cage. You fight until one gives up. The winner gets half the money that is bet, while the men running the fights kept the rest."

"So underground fighting."

"Yes." I took a breath. "And I was good. Small in

those days, but fast and strong. I learned quickly how to play dirty. Kicking out a knee, the kidneys, whatever it took to win. I had no choice."

"Oh, baby." She squeezed my free hand, tipping up her face to look at me as I continued.

"By the time I was fifteen, I had made a name for myself. Not just in the town where we lived, but back home in Siberia. People heard about Konstantin Volkov, the Siberian beast. My fists had become lethal and this was when the trouble began."

I took a breath, wondering how to condense a lifetime of pain and misery into a simple conversation for the woman I was falling in love with without scaring her off.

"It's okay," she said. "Whatever it is, you can tell me."

"You've heard of the Russian Mafia, the Bratva, things like this?"

"Sure."

"There was another faction—it's difficult to explain if you are not from there, but Mafia is easiest for conversation."

"Okay."

"There was a man. Dmitri. He ran everything dirty in Siberia and all the surrounding cities. He began sending a van for me every Friday night, bringing me to wherever he arranged big fights.

Higher stakes. More money. Women. Drugs. Anything we wanted. And I made a lot of money.

"During this time, Svetlana had had enough with her father and left home, but had nowhere to go. She was living on the streets, sleeping with rich, powerful men who would give her a room for the night, a meal, whatever she could get out of them. We were not a couple, you understand? We were just two scared, inexperienced teenagers with nothing to look forward to in life who found comfort and friendship together."

Lucy was listening quietly, so I kept going before I chickened out.

"My life changed just before I turned sixteen. This night, my grandmother came and gave me money—everything she had. Told me to have Svetlana bet it all on me for the upcoming fight. When I won—and I had never lost so it wasn't even a question at that point—I wouldn't have to fight anymore because we would get five times the original bet. She wanted me to focus on hockey.

"Dmitri, who ran the fights, also wanted Svetlana. He'd tried to claim her many times, but he was three times her age, and she knew firsthand how rough and dangerous he could be. Normally, she stayed away from the fights because of him, but she came that night to place my grandmother's bet. She disappeared once we got there, and Dmitri called me to his office. He told me he needed me to lose. That he would give me more money for losing than I would make by winning."

"Oh no."

"And there was no way to tell him what my grandmother had done or to stop Svetlana from making the bet. It turned out my opponent was Dmitri's illegitimate son and the boy's mother, Dmitri's mistress, begged him to let her son think he could beat me. So there was nothing I could do but agree."

"Did you lose?"

I slowly shook my head. "No. I couldn't bring myself to lose my grandmother's money. I figured they wouldn't kill me since I couldn't make money for them if I was dead, but at least my grandmother would be okay. And I foolishly thought maybe they would only break my leg or something."

"Oh, Kon." Her blue eyes were filled with worry.

"But they *were* going to kill me," I continued wearily. I hated thinking about this story, much less telling it to someone else. "They dragged me out after the fight and brought me to a back room. I was…tied up and being beaten with a metal pipe by several men. And then Svetlana came. Somehow, she found out what was going on, and she offered herself to Dmitri—to do anything he wanted to her for as long as he wanted—in exchange for my life."

Lucy sucked in a breath. "Oh my god."

"And he agreed."

"Holy shit."

"It took me six months to find her. And when I saw what he'd done to her…" My voice trailed off as I tried not to think about the condition that I'd found her in. "I killed him."

CHAPTER TWENTY-THREE

Lucy

"I wasn't expecting this," I told Kon the next morning as I scanned the contents of his refrigerator.

It was cleaner and more organized than any refrigerator I'd ever seen. Fresh fruits and veggies were sorted into glass containers. He had eggs, butter, bacon, and cream—everything I needed to make us a good breakfast.

"What were you expecting?" he asked, approaching me from behind and putting a hand on the curve of my ass.

"Well, Sawyer had beer, bologna, and mustard when I got to his house. Something more like that, I guess."

He laughed softly against my neck, kissing me until I forgot the contents of the fridge and sank back against him.

"It will sound strange to you, but one of my dreams growing up was a refrigerator like this. Always full of food. My housekeeper knows what I like and she makes sure I always have it."

He wrapped his arms around me from behind. I'd woken up later than usual after our late night and we'd had morning sex and snuggled. Around eleven, he'd made coffee and brought me some in bed. I could have stayed there with him all day, but we were hungry and it was almost noon, so I'd put on one of his T-shirts and ventured into the kitchen.

"That doesn't sound strange at all," I said. "I know my reasons aren't the same as yours, but I find a clean house and a stocked fridge very comforting."

"What can I do to help?" he asked, releasing me from his hold.

"Can you grab the bacon, eggs, and cream? And those cherries, too. Where in the world did you get fresh cherries in St. Louis in early December, by the way?"

He shrugged. "My housekeeper gets everything."
"I like her."
After he had grabbed what I needed from the

fridge, I got mushrooms, an onion, and a block of cheddar cheese. As soon as I put everything on the counter, I took a moment to ogle Kon, who only wore a pair of black gym shorts. He was leaning his hip against the kitchen counter and sipping his coffee. God, he was ridiculous to look at. All defined muscles and ink.

"You look hungry," he said, smirking.

I laughed at the truth in his words.

"I'm not saying I don't want you again, because I definitely do. But I need to eat first."

"Me too. I don't think there's a single sperm left in my balls. You drained me dry, Miss Cain."

"I need a knife and a cutting board," I said. "And I believe it was you who woke me up with your dick pressed against my ass this morning, Mr. Volkov."

He opened a drawer and took out a wood cutting board, a smile playing on his lips.

"This is the risk you take when you sleep naked in my bed with an ass like that."

"I'll remember that."

He brought over a knife and a cutting board, kissing me. "How can I help with breakfast?"

I looked around at all the ingredients on the counter. "Why don't you crack some eggs into a bowl for me? Maybe six or seven."

He grinned. "I will eat at least that many on my own. I'll do the whole dozen."

I shook my head, unable to imagine eating as much as he did and still having abs. He burned a lot of calories playing hockey, of course, but it still seemed unfair.

As I laid the bacon in strips on a plate to cook it in the microwave, I cleared my throat and found Kon's gaze.

"Thank you for telling me what you did last night. It took a lot of courage to be that vulnerable."

His expression turned serious. "I am not proud of my past, but I want you to understand why I owe Svetlana."

"You have nothing to be ashamed of. And she owes you, too."

He looked down at the ground. "I can never go back to Russia because of what I did. And my grandmother refuses to leave. So I will never see her again."

"My dad used to say that *never* is never guaranteed. I don't mean to minimize what you're saying, because it has to feel terrible, but don't give up."

He shrugged. "She is happy. That is the most important thing. She has always been loyal to her country. And she is proud of me."

"Are you able to help her, even though you can't go there?"

"Yes. I pay people there to make sure she is taken care of. She does not know it. At least I don't think she does."

I finished with the bacon and washed my hands, then walked over and took his face in my hands.

"You're a good man, Konstantin Volkov. And there aren't many of those."

I kissed him and he put his hands on my hips.

"Thank you," he said. "You are a good woman, too. That is why I don't want you to leave. This thing between us…it's good, Lucy."

He leaned his forehead against mine and my pulse raced with awareness.

"It is," I whispered.

I closed my eyes, wishing this weekend could last forever. Here, we were safe. Nothing and no one could come between us. We had to leave his apartment eventually, though, and since he'd shared his deepest truths with me, I needed to do the same.

"When we sit down to eat," I said softly, "I'm going to tell you about Nate."

———

"I APPLIED for a job in customer service, but during the interview, Nate asked me to take the open position he had for an office manager," I said a few minutes later. "It was hard at first."

"Why?" Kon asked me, his food untouched as he listened to me.

"Because all the other women in the office thought they should have been hired as the office manager. I was their boss on my first day of work there." I gestured toward his plate. "Eat, please. I'm going to."

He took a bite of his omelet and nodded with appreciation. "Very good, Lucy."

I finished off a piece of bacon and continued. "So I made some changes to things in the office. I implemented more flexible hours and shorter workdays on Friday. I streamlined some things and started outsourcing some of the work for the people who had too much on their plates. And after a few months, I don't know if I'd say everyone liked me, but they didn't hate me anymore. Nate started asking me to stay late and help him with special projects, and I didn't realize at the time it was because he liked me."

Kon's jaw hardened and I decided to skip the details of this next part.

"So anyway, we started dating and after a few

months of dating I moved in with him. His house was closer to the office, and…" I shook my head. "I liked him well enough."

"Was that when he became abusive?" he asked.

"No. He actually…so here's what happened. As the office manager, I had full access to everything. I always had the accounts manager give me a listing of all incoming and outgoing expenses every month, so I knew how much we were spending on things. I was reading through that report one month and I saw that Nate had cut a check for $25,000 to someone, but there was no policy number tied to it. Every payment that goes out should have either a purchase order number or a policy number on it. Make sense?"

Kon nodded. "Yes."

"I almost asked him about it, but then…something just didn't feel right to me. He never cuts checks himself. He always asks the office manager to do it. So when he was out of town for a conference, I stayed late one night and did some digging. He had written the check to a man who had recently been released from prison for manslaughter."

Kon's brows shot up. "Oh, Lucy. This is bad."

I exhaled hard, taking a bite of my omelet before continuing.

"I got into Nate's locked drawer of files and spent

hours going through them. It took me a while to piece everything together, but I eventually figured out that one of our life insurance policyholders with a $1,000,000 policy had died a week after Nate wrote that check. The family never got paid out, though. Nate forged a cancellation letter dated a few months before and told the family the policyholder's policy had been canceled and he just never told them about it. He gave the home office—the insurance company he's an agent for—an account number that he said belonged to the family, but it was actually an account he had set up. He took that million dollars and kept it."

"Jesus." Kon's expression was a mix of worry and anger.

"Yeah. I was in shock, to be honest. I wanted to continue a deep dive into all his files, but he was coming back the next day and I couldn't risk it."

I remembered that night so well. Instead of sleeping, I'd stared at the ceiling for hours, sick over what Nate had done and thinking about how I stupidly would have gone on about life without knowing if I'd never seen that check and looked into it.

I blew out a breath, just thinking about it making my stomach tense into a knot.

"I had copies of what I'd found, but I needed more time. I decided to go on about life like I didn't know anything had happened and bide my time until I could check his phone when he was in the shower sometime and go through his paper files more thoroughly."

"Why?" Kon looked at me like I was crazy. "Why didn't you get the hell out of there?"

"I didn't have anything concrete connecting the man he'd paid the $25,000 to. I thought it was likely he had paid that guy to kill the policyholder so he could collect on the policy, but I didn't have proof." I set my fork down, suddenly not hungry. "That man was only forty-eight years old. He was a husband and a father. They didn't just lose him, they got screwed out of the insurance settlement that was rightfully theirs. I wanted to do right by them."

Kon reached across the table and took my hand. "I understand."

"What I didn't know is that Nate has a silent alarm on that locked drawer in his office," I said flatly. "So he knew I'd been in it. He confronted me about it at home and…" I looked away, tears forming in my eyes. "I tried to lie my way out of it, but I couldn't. He tried to justify what he did, said he needed the money to keep the office afloat, but it was a lie. The office was fine. Then he tried to bring me in on it. Told me that we could have ten million within a year and then disappear somewhere together."

Kon's eyes were wide with disbelief. "I had no idea it was…I am so sorry, Lucy. What did you say?"

I smiled. "I told him to go fuck himself. I realize now I should have played along until I could get out of there, but in that moment, I was…enraged. I hated him for being such a monster and I hated myself for being with him."

"You did nothing wrong," Kon said softly.

"I know, but…anyway, he ended up choking me."

Kon bowed his head.

We fought and I seriously thought he might kill me. I ended up pushing the button to trigger the home security system, which automatically calls the police. It's set up so that the 9-1-1 operator calls Nate's phone immediately, and if he doesn't answer, the police come to the house. So while he was on the phone trying to convince them everything was fine, I got out."

"And you never went back, right?"

I shook my head. "No. I borrowed some clothes and shoes from a friend and gave her some money to buy my bus ticket here. I have copies of everything and I planned to have them mailed to three different news reporters if anything ever happens to me. It's not that I mind him getting in trouble, but he told me that if anyone finds out about anything, he'll…" I swallowed hard, tears pooling in my eyes. "Have my mom and her sister killed."

"My god, Lucy." Kon scrubbed his hands down his face.

"So now you know," I said, my voice breaking with emotion.

He squeezed my hand, not saying anything. Not telling me everything was going to be okay. Just being there with me in the moment.

And I loved him for it.

CHAPTER TWENTY-FOUR

Kon

MY WEEKEND with Lucy was one of the best I'd ever spent with a woman. I'd had practice, but other than that, it was just the two of us. Talking, making love, just being together. We'd opened up about our pasts, creating a level of intimacy I'd never had with anyone else. Things would have been perfect if not for the fact that a criminal was after her, making her want to disappear. Not just from him, but from her entire life. Whether she took off for Europe or lived off the grid somewhere in the US, her future couldn't include me if she was on the run.

It had been a long time since I'd felt the urge to hurt someone. Sure, I'd wanted to pound the living shit out of Keegan, but that was different. Kicking a guy's ass or getting into fights on the ice was different than the rage that had fueled me the night I'd killed Dmitri. And my need to protect Lucy from the men threatening her brought it all back.

The worst part for me was not knowing.

I didn't know how to protect her when I was gone.

I didn't know what Nate was planning next.

I didn't even know if Sawyer was physically capable of protecting her when I couldn't.

And more than any of that, I didn't know what the fuck she and I were going to do moving forward. The only thing I'd gotten her to agree to was that she wouldn't leave without telling me. So basically, we were in a holding pattern.

I was grumpy about it as we got to the arena in Colorado for our morning skate. We'd left St. Louis yesterday and I'd spent most of the night tossing, turning, and worrying. The threat from Nate was real now that I knew the details. It scared me, which said something, because I wasn't the type of man who was easily frightened.

"Who pissed in your cornflakes?" Boone asked as I dropped down into a split, stretching out my legs. "You're even grumpier now than you were before you started hooking up with Lucy."

I narrowed my eyes. "We are not hooking up," I told him. "We are dating. Is not the same."

His eyebrows rose. "Yeah? You gettin' serious with Sawyer's sister?"

"For real?" Of course, Rory heard us and joined the conversation. "Damn, bro, you've got balls of steel, dating a teammate's sister."

I rolled my eyes at them. "We are adults. You are ridiculous."

"I would cut your balls off if it was my sister," Lars interjected from behind me.

I groaned, shaking my head.

"The bigger question," Nash said, skating up next to us, his face full of mischief. "Is what are you getting her for Christmas?"

Four pairs of eyes turned to me and I frowned. Why were they looking at me like that?

"Why are you looking at me like this?" I demanded, getting to my feet and rolling my neck.

"He has no clue," Boone said, laughing.

"Dude." Rory shook his head. "Even I know you gotta buy the girl you're currently getting horizontal with something for Christmas."

"We're new," I protested, looking from one to the other, an uneasy feeling washing through me. For Rory and Nash, the two biggest pranksters on the team, to be on board with whatever this was, it probably meant they were serious.

"Are they fucking with me?" I demanded from Boone when Coach blew the whistle, indicating we needed to start drills.

"A little," Boone nodded. "But only a little. Christmas is a big deal. Don't you celebrate Christmas?"

"Yes, but…" I wasn't sure how to explain my views on Christmas and religion. "We had no money for gifts or decorations or anything when I was growing up, and I don't practice any religion now."

"It doesn't have to be about religion," he said gently. "It's about family. Tradition. Friends. The thought you put into a special gift for a special person, whether it's your dad or your girlfriend or one of your kids. Lots of nonreligious people celebrate Christmas because it makes people feel good. That's why people donate so much to charity around the holidays too. At the risk of sounding like a sap, it's what's in here—" He tapped his gloved hand over his chest. "And it sounds to me like she's in there too." He winked and skated over to join his line.

"Don't let them get under your skin," Wes said, sitting beside me as he waited for one of our equipment managers to finish adjusting one of his skates.

"I don't know what to get her," I admitted. "I did not even think about Christmas."

"Well, you haven't been together long, so we're not talking about diamonds or anything like that. I think something more personal. Maybe plane tickets for the two of you to get away during the All-Star break, or something like that."

I didn't know where Lucy would be by the time February rolled around, but I couldn't say that to Wes.

"My main piece of advice is this," he said, getting up and testing his weight on his skate. "Don't listen when they say they don't want or need anything. Because even if it's true, they still want that surprise under the tree. Trust me on this. It's not about the money you spend, but the thought you put into it."

Fucking great.

I had tons of money.

I had much less in the way of creativity.

I was going to need some help coming up with the perfect gift for Lucy.

———

AFTER A FRUSTRATING LOSS IN COLORADO, we flew to San Jose. We'd just gotten to the arena when Coach

Gizzard came in followed by a familiar-looking man in a suit.

"Gentleman!" Coach whistled. "I'd like you to welcome Hudson Granger to the team. With Sawyer taking an extended bereavement leave, we've been light on defense. The trade went through this morning and he'll be in the lineup tonight. Please make him feel at home."

Coach turned and disappeared, leaving us to greet our new teammate.

I knew of him, of course. He'd come from Tampa and there were a lot of rumors around the league about him. Something about a motorcycle accident? I didn't pay much attention to gossip like that, so I wasn't sure that was the story I was thinking of. Hockey was like anything else when you got a large group of people together; everyone talked, everyone had opinions, and the truth was usually somewhere in the middle.

I took a minute to introduce myself and then hung back with Boone and Rory as Wes helped him settle in. It was early, so we had time before the game. I was curious about what changes Coach was going to make to the lines even though it wouldn't impact me. I wasn't even supposed to play tonight since I'd played the last four games in a row, but I still paid attention to any changes on the ice. It was important for me to stay on top of that kind of thing, so I had a feel for the different lines when they were on the ice.

"You think this means Sawyer's not coming back?" Boone asked under his breath as we finished changing.

"I hope not," I said. "Lucy told me he's been working out again, trying to get himself in shape. Why else would he do this if he didn't want to come back?"

"I think they're going to send Marsh back down," Rory said. "He hasn't had a point in weeks."

That made sense. Marsh had been called up from our minor league affiliate but hadn't been very successful so far this season. A guy like Granger could potentially be much more impactful on the ice.

"I think Granger's dad was one of the people who died on 9/11," Nash said quietly.

We all turned to look at him.

"Are you sure?" Boone asked.

"No." Nash shook his head. "But I feel like someone mentioned it somewhere."

"Probably not something we can just randomly ask," Boone said, grimacing.

We stood around for a while, wasting time while we waited for dinner to arrive. Food was always provided on game nights, but most of us liked to order specific meals and they never arrived at the same time. Since I had a little time, I dug out my phone and texted Lucy.

Kon: Hello, beautiful.

Lucy: Hey, handsome.

Kon: I just wanted you to know I'm thinking about you.

Lucy: I've been thinking of you too. Where are you?

Kon: The arena in San Jose, waiting for my dinner to arrive.

Lucy: Eating anything good?

Kon: Nothing as good as your chicken and dumplings.

Lucy: I can arrange to have chicken and dumplings ready when you get back.

Kon: I am a lucky man.

Lucy: You're lucky I love to cook. Anyway, good luck in the game tonight. You're not playing, though, right?

Kon: Not unless Coach makes a last-minute change. How did you know?

Lucy: Sawyer has hockey on the TV 24/7 and I heard it on one of the pregame shows. It's all Sawyer watches these days.

Kon: Maybe this is good. To get him excited to play again.

Lucy: I hope so. He's been running five miles almost every day.

Kon: He is making good progress. Maybe after Christmas he can start to practice with the team again.

Lucy: You think that soon? Christmas is only a few weeks away.

Kon: Speaking of Christmas...is it a big celebration for you? Are you religious? I was thinking maybe we could spend the holidays together, but I am not religious, so I wanted to ask you what your plans are with your family.

Lucy: This is going to be Sawyer's first without Annie, so I'm a little stressed about it. They hosted every year and whatever family was available would fly out. Annie's family would always be there, and then Mom and I would also join. I don't know what's happening this year, but we're not very religious either. Sawyer and Annie used to go to service on Christmas Eve, but I haven't gone in years. It's more about spending time with the family, you know?

Kon: We never did anything in Russia, so this is only my second time officially celebrating Christmas. I'm not sure about all the celebrations here in the US.

Lucy: Then we should do all the things you've never done. Have you ever decorated a tree?

Kon: I bought a pre-decorated tree and Mayra puts it up.

Lucy: Can you see me rolling my eyes over here? You can help me and Sawyer decorate ours when you get back from your trip.

Lucy: We can bake cookies, too.

Lucy: Oh! And watch Christmas movies...have you ever seen "A Christmas Story"?

Lucy: And don't forget Christmas shopping!

I chuckled at the texts popping up one at a time.

My girl was into Christmas.

Which meant I was about to get into it too.

I didn't care how far out of my comfort zone all of this was—I'd do anything she asked of me if it meant keeping her around.

CHAPTER TWENTY-FIVE

Lucy

I scowled at the laptop screen when I saw my current checking account balance. Not working wasn't sustainable for me.

If I cashed out my retirement fund, which was my plan, I'd be able to start fresh. Still, it wasn't a ton of money, and I hated the thought of spending every dollar I had to my name.

Sawyer was out on his run, and it was the perfect time to go check out the only idea I had for a part-time job—Morelli Brothers. There was a *Help Wanted* sign in their window, and I couldn't imagine better people to work for.

Leaving here was going to be hard, and I was more

undecided about it than ever because things were going so well with Kon. Sawyer was doing great, too, and being roommates had turned out to be a good fit for us.

I grabbed the keys to Sawyer's SUV and my bag, checking to make sure the cards were in there. It was nearly impossible to find the right gift for people who had put their lives on the line for you, but I'd gotten each of them a gift card to a local Italian restaurant. It wasn't much, but the gifts and the heartfelt thanks I'd written in each card were better than just saying thank you.

Before I opened the garage door, I locked myself in the car and took my new pepper spray from my bag and put it within arm's reach. Leaving the house alone was risky, but I refused to let Nate make me into a terrified prisoner.

After a deep breath to ground myself, I opened the garage door and backed out. I could do this. I'd park close to the door and ninja my way in there, pepper spray in hand.

Or something. I'd spent a lot of money on holiday gifts—at least a lot for me—and I couldn't just sit at home like a damsel in distress as my bank account dwindled.

The Morellis had started selling holiday baked goods yesterday morning, and I was hoping they'd be extra busy and hire me instantly because they were desperate for extra help. My jaw dropped as I passed the bakery entrance and saw a line that went out the door and halfway down the block.

Holy shit. I usually got here early in the morning, normally before seven, but today it was closer to nine. I didn't know if the crowd was due to the later hour or the holiday items, but I was happy for my friends.

Parking in front of the store was impossible, so I parked a block over, got my pepper spray in hand, and ran to the front door.

"Hey, there's a line!" a woman snapped at me.

"Oh, I'm..." I considered what to say without pissing anyone off. "Not a customer."

At least, I didn't feel like one anymore. Not only had the Morellis saved my life, they'd also become very special to me. I looked forward to my visits to the bakery when I got to talk to them, and I felt like I was getting to know each of them.

I worked my way through the crowd and went to the front counter, catching Luigi's attention.

"Lucy!" he cried as he swiped a customer's debit card. "How are you?"

"Doing great." I slid out of my coat. "I came to ask about your help wanted sign in the window."

His whole face lit up and he pointed at me. "You? You want to work here?"

I nodded. "If you need me, I'm in."

"Lucy, you're an angel! Can you start this very second?"

Shrugging, I said, "Sure."

"Go wash up in back and find Mario. He'll put you to work."

I had a job! And it involved baking, which was something I loved. But I didn't have time to celebrate the moment. As soon as I'd dropped my coat and bag in the office and washed my hands, Mario greeted me and showed me how to bake bread. I had a huge spatula thing that I moved the loaves in and out of the ovens with, and once they'd cooled, I put them in bags and wrapped each bag with a foil twist tie.

"Lucy, welcome to the family!" Maria said, looking up from her station, where she was decorating cookies.

"Thanks, I'm so happy to be here."

"How are you doing?" she asked.

"Good."

"Have they caught the guy who attacked you?"

I shook my head. There was no hope of that, but I didn't mention it to her.

"Don't you walk out of here alone," she said,

pointing at me. "One of us will walk you to your car later."

It was a touching gesture, but I had no intention of being the cause of Luigi hurting his knee again, or Mario testing the limits of his heart with a sprint. A shot in anyone's eyes with my pepper spray would give me enough time to get away.

I was sweating and covered in a thin layer of flour when I realized after about an hour that I hadn't told Sawyer where I was.

"Hey, I need to let my brother know I'm here," I said to Mario. "Is that okay?"

"Of course." He lowered his brows, studying my wool sweater. "Hey, do you want a T-shirt to change into?"

I laughed as I wiped my forearm across my brow. "More than anything."

He found a gray "Morelli Brothers" T-shirt in the back, and I changed before sending a quick text to my brother, then got back to baking bread. It was a few minutes after noon when things finally started to slow down.

"Lucy, go get some lunch," Luigi said. "Great job this morning."

"Thanks." I took off the apron I'd been wearing all morning. "Is there a place close by that's good for picking up a sandwich?"

"We provide lunch. Unless you want something gluten vegan whatever." He rolled his eyes. "But if a good deli sandwich and some amazing salt and vinegar chips will do, just go make a plate in the break room. Lunch is half an hour."

"Thanks."

It was nice to be part of something again. I'd been bored a lot at Sawyer's house, and now that he was doing better, I didn't need to be there all the time anymore.

In the break room, I met several other employees and filled out some employment paperwork after I'd eaten a roast beef sandwich. The break room was decked out with news articles about the Morelli Brothers bakery, and I discovered that Mario was actually a decorated war hero.

"Can you come back tomorrow?" Luigi asked me when I returned to the huge, open work area.

"Sure, what time?"

He chuckled. "Whenever you want. We're so understaffed we'll take anything."

"You tell me when, and I'll be here."

"Could you do five a.m.? Until about one p.m.?"

"Sure."

He grinned. "Great. We're so happy to have you on board, Lucy. You fit right in here."

————

I LEFT the bakery a few hours later feeling light. On the walk to my car, I texted Kon.

Lucy: I got a job! At Morelli Brothers bakery. I hope you find the smell of cookies sexy. I'll tell you all about it later. xoxo

The bakery had been full of holiday spirit—literally. I'd swept large piles of red and green sprinkles from the floor before leaving. Tomorrow Maria was going to show me how to decorate cookies, and I looked forward to doing something other than baking bread for my entire shift.

When I got to Sawyer's car, I pushed the button on the key fob to unlock it and opened the door. I didn't make it inside, though, because I was pulled backward and a hand was clamped over my mouth.

My heart hammered as I fumbled with my pepper spray. I held it over my head and pressed the button, but it was knocked from my hand.

I already had two massive arms wrapped around me, so that hand meant there was more than one person. My heart sank. Like last time, I kicked and writhed and tried everything in my power to get free, but this guy was much bigger and stronger than the last one.

Within seconds, I was tossed into the back of a

van, where two men waited. I sucked in a breath, desperate for air now that there was no hand over my mouth, and the van's doors slammed behind me.

It started moving immediately.

"Don't try to get smart," one of the men said. "Give me your hands and this will all go easier."

I sighed heavily, about to give in when the other man slapped me across the face hard enough to make my head spin.

"That's for what you did to my hand, bitch." He took off his dark ski mask and I recognized him as the man who had attacked me in the alley.

"That's right," I held his gaze. "You're the scary guy who hurts senior citizens."

The other man gave him a confused look. "What did you do?"

"Shut the fuck up and tie her hands."

The first guy scoffed. "Don't forget who's in charge here. It's not you. You botched this last time."

"Fuck off."

"Don't hit her again," the first man said. "You know our orders."

Were they not supposed to hurt me? That gave me a shred of hope. I didn't know if Nate had told these guys to bury me alive in a deep hole somewhere or to bring me to him.

Either way, I was screwed. The thought of a

painful death sent me into a complete panic, though. I had so much to live for.

As I let my hands be tied, I looked around, hoping to find something that could help me.

"Looking for your purse?" the second guy asked me.

"No one calls them purses anymore, asshole. And you should seriously reconsider the length of your mustache."

The first guy snickered. Mustache's scowl was murderous.

"Your *purse* is gone, smartass," he muttered. "So is your phone. Unless you've got some more broken-down old guys on the way to save your ass, it's over for you."

He had the upper hand here, but I wouldn't allow anyone to insult my friends on my watch.

"Those old guys are ten times the men you'll ever be," I fired back.

"Okay, sparky, I need to tie your ankles now," the man who had just finished tying my hands said.

Tears pooled in my eyes. I was in a bad situation, but I didn't think I could just lie here and let him tie my ankles. If I could get the van door open when we were stopped at a light, I had a chance of running.

How would I get the door open with my hands tied, though?

"You guys, my brother is a pro hockey player," I said. "Whatever Nate's paying you, my brother will pay you a lot more to take me to him."

"That decision is above our pay grade," the nicer one said. "Ankles."

Mustache pulled me into his lap and held on to my upper body as I kicked the other one. It was no use, though. He had my ankles bound with wire in less than a minute.

This was really bad, but I had to keep my wits about me. I had to be ready to grab any chance at escape, no matter how impossible it seemed.

All hope wouldn't be lost until I wasn't breathing anymore. And I still had an ace in my pocket—or rather, tucked into my bra. I'd placed my new AirTag there when I got dressed this morning. If I could keep them from discovering it until Sawyer realized I was missing, he'd be able to track my location with it.

CHAPTER TWENTY-SIX

Kon

WE GOT HOME from our road trip late in the afternoon and though I wanted to see Lucy right away, I wanted to shower and change first. Lucy was making the chicken and dumplings she'd promised me tonight and invited me to join her and Sawyer for dinner before she and I headed back to my place. We were trying to find a balance between spending as much time together as possible, and not abandoning Sawyer now that he was doing so much better. Luckily, Sawyer had been one of my closest friends before I met Lucy, so I liked spending time with him. I just hoped nothing would change now that she and I were involved.

I was curious to hear about this new job she'd found too. For selfish reasons, I hoped it was something she loved so it would keep her here in St. Louis.

With me.

I'd spent a lot of time in the last few days thinking about how to deal with the situation with her ex. Sawyer and I both had money, so we could potentially pay the guy off. If he was a crook, he was motivated by money, right? Most people were. And everyone had a price. At least in Russia they did. Maybe it was different here. At some point, I needed to talk to Sawyer about all of that. He couldn't want her to go into hiding any more than I did, so maybe between us we could find a way to help her.

Deep down, I wanted her to stay for me, but I understood fear and intimidation. Especially the threat to her mother and aunt. I was going to handle it, though. One way or another. I didn't have a plan yet, but that was why I needed to talk to Sawyer. Maybe I could convince him to work out with me one day next week, and we could talk without Lucy there. Not that I was trying to go behind her back, but I figured she would be uncomfortable with the idea of me bribing Nate.

I sent her a quick text telling her I was on the way before getting in my truck.

"Hey." Sawyer opened the door with a weird look on his face as he peered behind me. "Is Lucy with you?"

I frowned. "With me? I just got back from the airport," I said. "I stopped to shower and change, but she invited me to dinner so I came right over."

"She got a job working over at the Morelli's Brothers bakery but they close at two and it's…" He looked at his watch. "After four."

I pulled out my phone and noted the text I'd sent her didn't show that it had been read.

"Have you called her?" I asked him.

He shook his head. "She sounded super excited about this new job so I figured she was hanging out with the Morellis and then maybe going over to your place since she has my truck."

We looked at each other and something sour twisted in my gut.

I yanked out my phone and called her, but it went straight to voice mail.

"I'm going to call the bakery, just in case she's still there." Sawyer said, pulling out his phone and putting it on speaker. "Maybe they're working late or something."

"This is Luigi." Luigi Morelli had a much deeper voice than I'd expected.

"Mr. Morelli. This is Sawyer Cain. Lucy's brother."

"Oh, hello, Sawyer! Lucy talks about you all the time."

"Is Lucy still there?" he asked.

"Lucy left a couple of hours ago," Luigi said slowly. "She didn't come home?"

"Fuck." Sawyer swung a panicked gaze in my direction and fear crawled down my spine.

"I'm gonna call my daughter," Luigi said. "See if Lucy said anything to her about her plans. I'll call you back."

"Thank you." Sawyer disconnected and we stared at each other.

"This is bad," I said needlessly.

"She has my truck," Sawyer said. "I can call LoJack and they'll tell me where it is."

It felt like an eternity as Sawyer talked to the customer service person who could access the GPS in his truck. Luigi called us back, but no one from the bakery had any idea where Lucy might have gone after she left for the day.

"My truck is parked two blocks from the bakery," Sawyer said. "Let's go."

We raced out of the house, and I broke every speeding law known to man as I drove to the bakery.

Sawyer's truck was right where they'd told him it

was. The doors were unlocked and the driver's side door wasn't completely closed.

"This is Lucy's," I said, picking up a canister of pepper spray a few feet away from the truck.

"We have to call the police," Sawyer said, reaching for his phone.

"She's only been gone a few hours," I told him. "They won't do anything. For all they know, she went shopping."

"But—" he began.

"I know!" I hissed. "But I'm telling you, the police won't help. We have to find her on our own. Do you know how to reach Nate?"

"I've got his number, yeah."

"Call him. Ask him what he wants for Lucy."

Sawyer's gaze hardened. "You think…"

"Stop wasting time," I growled. "We both know he did this. Find out what he wants."

Sawyer picked up his phone and then hesitated. "Lucy said he threatened my mom and aunt. He said he would kill them if she told anyone what he did."

"She has evidence about what he did, yes?" I asked, thinking back to what she'd told me.

"Yeah, it's hidden in the house, but I know where it is."

"Call your mother while we go back to your house," I said abruptly. "We have to make sure the evidence is safe. If they get that, we have no leverage and no way to prove he's after her."

"Shit!"

We separated, with him getting in his truck and me getting in mine.

I didn't know what we were going to do, but no matter what, we needed help. The police wouldn't do shit until we either had proof she'd been taken or she'd been missing for forty-eight hours. I didn't plan to wait that long.

"Yo." Boone answered on the first ring. "What's wrong? You didn't get enough of my charming personality the last week? You need more Boone time?"

"Lucy is missing. Can you meet me at Sawyer's?"

"Wha—are you serious? I'm on my way."

"Call Wes," I said before disconnecting.

This was a disaster and with every passing moment, I was more terrified than I'd ever been in my life. I had no idea what Nate or his men might be doing to her, and if they hurt one hair on her head, I would end all of them.

———

BOONE, Rory, and Wes pulled up to Sawyer's house within five minutes of us getting home. Sawyer was on the phone with his mother, so I filled the others in on what was going on.

"Give me the papers," Wes said immediately. "Whoever these people are, they don't know me beyond being one of Sawyer's teammates, so I'm not going to be the first place they look. I also have a safe-deposit box I can still get to right now. My bank is open for another thirty minutes."

"Sawyer!" I motioned for him to look at me. "Lucy's papers—get them now."

Sawyer ran up the stairs and came down a minute later, handing over a large envelope while it appeared he was trying to convince his mother to move to a hotel for a few nights.

"Mom, I don't have time to argue with you," he was saying. "Can you just do this for me? Please?"

"I'm going to get these papers to a safe place," Wes said.

"I'm coming with you," Rory said. "Just in case someone's watching or tries to follow you."

"Let's go."

The two of them left and I looked at Boone. "I will destroy every one of them if they hurt her."

"I know, buddy." He nodded, his usual playfulness nowhere to be found. "And I'll be right there with you."

"Okay." Sawyer finally hung up. "Mom and Aunt

Sue are going to a hotel under an assumed name. I talked to the hotel, told them who I was and that a stalker had been threatening my family. They assured me no one would know Mom's real identity. It's not perfect, but hopefully it'll slow Nate down long enough to get Lucy back."

"Call this fuckhead," Boone grumbled. "Let's get this show on the road."

"If we just—" I stopped talking as Sawyer smacked himself in the forehead.

"Jesus fucking Christ! I've been in such a panic, I totally forgot."

"What?" I demanded, glaring at him.

"The *AirTag*. Lucy got a fucking AirTag."

"A what?" I asked in confusion.

"It's a tracking device," Boone said, his eyes narrowing. "People usually use them to find keys and stuff, but if Lucy has one on her…"

"I thought she said she was putting it into her bra or something," Sawyer said, grabbing his phone and typing something in. "Holy shit. I found her."

"What does it say?" I demanded, getting more and more frustrated by the second.

"Her AirTag says she's about thirty minutes from here, in that industrial area near the river."

"Let's go." I turned toward the door but Boone grabbed my arm.

"Wait." His eyes met mine. "I know you're scared. I am too. But we can't just go in there without a plan. We don't know how many people there are or what condition she's in. Maybe we should try the police anyway?"

"I'm not waiting for them to get their heads out of their asses," I snapped. "They're going to ask us a million questions, and we do not have time for this. Come or do not come but give me the address."

"Okay, Boone's right." Sawyer stood on my other side. "We need a plan and backup. I think I should call Nate, let him believe we're willing to trade the papers or money or whatever he wants for Lucy. He doesn't know we know where she is, so we have the advantage. Come on, Kon. I want to get her back safe and as quickly as possible too, but we're no good to her dead."

"Call him," I said in a steely voice. "Because I am going to get her. One way or another."

CHAPTER TWENTY-SEVEN

Lucy

"CHRIST, this place stinks. Couldn't Max have found an old warehouse that didn't smell like pig shit?"

My kidnappers were complete amateurs. There were four men keeping me captive, and I already knew three of their names and had memorized the license plate of the van they drove me here in.

"I have to use the money for this job to pay my fucking taxes," Mustache said to the guy next to him. "I wanted to buy a boat, but the IRS has their dick up my ass again."

I probably could have gotten him to tell me his social security number if not for the gag in my mouth. A gag my captors had picked up from the ground of this filthy warehouse that stank of chemicals.

As a fairly average person, I'd never imagined myself getting kidnapped. That was something I'd only read about in books and seen in movies. But it had happened, and I was surprised by my reaction. I wasn't shaking and begging for my life; I was pissed.

I wasn't the asshole here. Nate was, hands down, the asshole and he continued to make my life a living hell. This cut-rate crew hadn't killed me yet, and I figured if they planned to, they would have done it already.

There was a problem, though, and it was a big one. These guys had a lot of guns. I'd seen more than ten different guns already. If Sawyer and Kon came running in here to save me, one of them could get shot. I wouldn't be able to live with myself if anything happened to one of them because they were trying to save me from Nate.

Actually, there was another problem. They'd bound my hands and ankles with wire. My wrists were already rubbed raw from what little struggling I'd done. I wasn't going to be able to free myself like people always did in the movies.

The only chance I had of getting out of this was by talking my way out of it. I made noises that came out muffled by the gag in my mouth until one of my captors came over to me. He was wiry and wore a gray hoodie.

"I can't understand you. What was that?" he said with a grin.

Hilarious. He was a kidnapper-slash-comedian. I continued with my noises until he untied the gag.

"Hey," I said, trying to sound friendly. "If you check my ID, you'll see that my name is Lucy Cain. My brother is Sawyer Cain, and he plays hockey for the Mavericks."

"What the fuck?" Mustache said with a sneer. "That's my team. I didn't know"

Hoodie silenced him with a glare.

"Do you need to piss or something?" he asked me.

"Yes," I lied. "And I also wanted to tell you that whatever you're getting paid, my brother will pay you a lot more."

He shook his head as he unwrapped the wire binding my wrists.

"He's a multimillionaire," I said, my wrists burning. "Nate is just a small-time local insurance agent. Sawyer can pay you guys money that will change your lives."

"I think we should listen to her," Mustache said.

Hoodie ignored him, freeing my hands and ankles. I cringed as I saw the damage to the skin around my wrists.

"You assholes wrapped her too tight," Hoodie said.

"I didn't want her to get away," someone said.

Two guns were pointed at me as Hoodie led me over to a large machine.

"Go behind there and piss," he said. "Try to run and we'll shoot you."

"So you have no interest in more money?" I asked him. "I could call my brother now and it could be in your account within an hour."

I could tell he was considering it. I didn't want to spend Sawyer's money, but if this worked, I knew he'd be okay with it.

Since I didn't really have to pee, I went behind the massive machine that looked like an old printing press and took a few deep breaths. There had to be a way out of this. Or at least a way to buy time.

"You about done?" Hoodie asked.

"Yes." I went back to where he stood. "Thanks for letting me pee. I can tell you're a reasonable man."

He scowled. "Don't try to butter me up, lady."

I sighed, feeling defeated. "Can you at least not put the wires back on? I'll sit down and you guys can point your guns at me."

"Yeah, whatever." He gestured with his gun in the direction of my other captors.

I sat down in the dirt, grateful I at least still had

my AirTag. It was starting to get darker, which meant it was probably close to five in the evening or so. Surely Sawyer would call the police and tell them where I was?

That was the smart play, but I had a bad feeling he'd show up here himself, with Kon. And knowing what I did about Kon's past, I was afraid he'd come in here with guns—or fists—blazing. That was too risky. They needed to leave that part to the police.

We'd been sitting in silence for a few minutes when the sound of voices made all of us turn. I held my breath, hoping it was the police but doubting cops would carry on a conversation in a situation like this.

When the two men appeared, the knot in my stomach doubled in size. It was Nate and his brother, Eric.

"Hey, Lucy," Nate said, grinning. "Fancy seeing you here."

Asshole. I didn't even look at him. His brother was a police officer who was risking his career to help his crooked sibling. I just hoped all of this would eventually catch up with both of them.

"We've got a big problem," Nate said. "But I guess you already know that."

I pressed my lips together, forcing away my urge to tell him what I was really thinking. I had to be smart. Maybe if I could make him think I was cooperating, he'd finally leave me alone.

"I'll return the papers," I offered. "Will that end all of this?"

He laughed and looked at his brother. "She'll return the papers. Then everything will be fine, won't it?"

Nate's fist connected with my jaw before I even realized it was coming. I found myself flat on the ground with dirt in my mouth, my face throbbing with pain.

"Hey, man," Mustache said. "You know who her brother is, right?"

"I don't give a fuck about her brother," Nate snarled.

"We're going to need to renegotiate," Hoodie said. "You didn't tell us who her brother was. This job was a lot higher risk than we thought."

"Talk to Max about that," Eric said. "Our deal is with him."

"Yeah, well Max isn't here, is he?" Hoodie shot back.

"You want to go all hot shit on us, copper?" someone yelled. "We've got a hell of a lot more guns than you do."

"Hey, take it easy," Nate said. "I'll double whatever Max promised you."

"Double?" Hoodie laughed. "I'd rather take the hockey player's money and let you two rot."

Movement by some tarp-covered machinery nearby made me move the hair from my face so I could get a better view.

I squinted, trying to make out what I was seeing in the dim light of the warehouse. My heart raced when I made out the face crouched down next to a machine.

It was Kon. He was dressed in such dark clothing that I could only make out his face. He brought a finger to his lips, telling me to keep quiet.

Which, obviously, I would. I got back into a sitting position and nodded.

"I liked it better when you were on the ground," Nate cracked, kicking my shoulder.

I sprawled into the dirt again, and all hell broke loose.

CHAPTER TWENTY-EIGHT

Kon

BACK WHEN I'D been fighting two or three nights a week, in the moments just before entering the cage, I would mentally retreat into a calm, quiet place inside of myself. It was how I'd centered my emotions so none of it was ever personal. The things I did were never about anything but the fight.

That wasn't going to work tonight because this was very, very personal. Seeing Nate kick Lucy had nearly sent me into a rage, but Boone's hand on my arm, reminding me of the guns these men had, kept me from losing my shit too soon. Because there was no doubt I was going to lose my shit.

There were only four of us since Lars and Wes

both had pregnant wives at home and we weren't willing to risk their lives too. However, Boone had refused to stay behind, and Rory met up with us after he and Wes left the bank. Having been a loner my entire life, I was beginning to realize just how good it was to have friends. Especially these men.

Sawyer had called the police just as we'd pulled up. He'd given them a brief synopsis of what had happened and told the person he spoke to he was going to try to reason with Nate. Then he'd given them the address and disconnected, leaving his phone in the truck. Hopefully, the name Sawyer Cain would alert someone's attention, but either way, Wes already had his attorney on standby. Just in case one or all of us wound up in jail. Probably me, because I was going to hurt someone in the very near future, but I didn't care.

I'd do whatever was necessary to rescue Lucy and take the fall if necessary, so my friends didn't have to.

"Hey, Nate." Sawyer took the lead, stepping out from behind a dumpster, hands in the air. It was risky for him to surprise them like that, but we'd all agreed it was the best way to distract everyone. If we rushed in together, and bullets started flying, people could die. Including Lucy, who was on the floor.

Nate and his men all swung around in surprise,

guns drawn, and I practically held my breath. We'd arranged ourselves so Sawyer could provide the distraction and then, hopefully, we'd be able to disarm and subdue them before they realized what we were doing.

"What the fuck are you doing here?" Nate asked with a growl, narrowing his eyes.

"Your first mistake was taking my sister," Sawyer responded in a calm, level voice. "Did you really think I'd sit back and let you hurt her? Or that I didn't put a tracker on her as soon as she told me what was going on? You must think I'm some dumb jock."

"Jesus fucking Christ." Some douchebag with a mustache huffed out a breath. "Are you serious, Nate? What the hell did you do?"

"Shut your fucking mouth," Nate hissed before turning back to Sawyer. "Technically, you kind of are a dumb jock because…" He motioned to his men. "There are a lot more of us than there are of you."

"Your second mistake," Sawyer continued, completely unamused, "was assuming I came alone."

Nate laughed. "Fuck you, Sawyer. You think I don't know when a man is bluffing? You and your pansy-ass athlete friends wouldn't know a gun from a hockey stick. And your stupid, spoiled, nosy bitch of a sister should've been happy to get married and let me knock her up. Instead, she had to poke around in things that had nothing to do with her. Now you're both going to die. But not until you tell me what you did with those papers."

"Already with my attorney," Sawyer said with a shrug. "Anything happens to either Lucy or me, and he goes straight to the cops. You're going to jail, Nate. Your brother too."

"You dumb motherfucker!" Mustache threw up his arms in frustration. "This was a half-assed operation run by a bunch of fucking—"

The man I'd figured out was Nate's brother Eric turned and fired his gun, shooting Mustache in the chest. Mustache fell back with a thud, eyes and mouth still wide with surprise.

This was escalating faster than I'd anticipated, so we had to do something before anything else happened that we couldn't control.

"Now!" I yelled.

All of us moved at once. I came out from behind the dumpster where I'd been hiding with a flying leap, taking out Nate and the guy next to him at the same time. I dug my elbow into Nate's head while kicking the gun from the other guy's hand. I couldn't see what the others were doing, because someone had jumped on my back and smacked me in the head with the butt of a gun, but it would take more than that to take me down.

"Get the guns!" I heard Sawyer yell.

"Fuck." I grunted as Eric fired off a round of shots that bounced off the metal containers in the room, splintering wood and drywall and god only knew what else. I heard Lucy's panicked scream and yelled out to her. "Run, Lucy!"

"I'll kill her!" Eric's voice rang out and time seemed to stop as I turned to see him holding Lucy by the hair, the gun pointed at her head.

"You won't kill anyone," Sawyer hissed, holding out a gun of his own and pointing it at Nate.

I jumped to my feet, yanking Nate up with me. I held him by the arm, fixing my gaze on Eric.

"You have three seconds to let her go," I said in an eerily calm voice.

Eric laughed. "Yeah, like I'm gonna just let her go because you said so."

"I wouldn't test him," Rory said, wiping a streak of blood from his cheek, his booted foot on the stomach of one of the kidnappers. "He's Russian and kinda crazy. I mean, I'm pretty crazy and he scares *me* so..."

"Two seconds," I said quietly, meeting Sawyer's eyes.

We'd only been friends a little over a year.

We'd bonded as his wife had been dying.

We had nothing in common beyond hockey and now Lucy.

And yet, Sawyer knew exactly what I was going to do and when I was going to do it. We didn't have to communicate verbally for me to trust he would do what needed to be done, no matter what happened to me.

"Dude, I would listen to him," Boone said, taking a step closer, as if he too understood what was about to happen.

"Fuck all of you," Eric laughed again. "I'm going to blow her pretty little brains all over this dirty warehouse as soon as—"

"Time's up." Without waiting for him to finish whatever he was going to say, I crouched low and launched myself toward the small area where I would make as much contact as possible with Eric without fully impacting Lucy. I went for the hand with the gun, throwing all my weight on that arm as Lucy dropped and scuttled out of the way.

Eric was stronger than he looked, and we rolled around on the filthy floor, each of us vying for control of the gun. I saw in my peripheral vision that Sawyer and Nate were also scuffling, but my gut told me Eric was the scarier of the two brothers. Their accomplices had already been subdued, and it was time to end this.

Even though it meant letting go of the arm with the gun, I knew I was faster than this prick. Drawing back my fist as I moved, I punched Eric hard enough to stun him. The gun clattered out of his hand and Boone rushed forward to grab it, but I didn't stop.

I *couldn't* stop.

There had been a time when my fists had kept me alive. Now they were going to keep Lucy and my friends alive and make one of the men who'd hurt her pay. Eric tried to fight back, but he was no match for me. Once I started hitting him, my body remembered what it was like to be fighting for my life. For Svetlana's life. My grandmother's. And I just kept hitting him. Over and over and over. Until blood spurted from his nose, then his mouth, and when I caught him on the side of his face, two teeth came out when he coughed.

"Kon!" Boone's voice penetrated my subconscious, but my body had a mind of its own. "The cops are here!"

"Kon!" I felt someone's hands on me. "He's out cold! It's over. Let him go."

I shook them off, swinging again and again, determined to make sure this fucker never hurt anyone ever again.

But now there was another voice.

And this one penetrated my haze of fury.

It was softer.

Crying.

Lucy.

"Konstantin. Babe. Don't. Please stop before the—"

"Police! Freeze!"

Boone tackled me, knocking me over and landing on top of me. I caught myself just before I punched him in the gut, suddenly remembering who and where I was.

"Easy, Killer," Boone said with a chuckle. "We got them. The cops are here. Your girl is safe. But let's not go to jail tonight, okay?"

My girl was safe.

I swung my eyes to Lucy, who was now in Sawyer's arms sobbing.

Jesus. Fucking. Christ.

What had I done?

What had I let her *see* me do?

The fight drained out of me and I let myself relax against the hard floor, Boone beside me as the cops swarmed around us. They were yelling and shouting orders, but I closed my eyes, waiting for the inevitable crash. Once the adrenaline left my body, it would hit me hard. And tomorrow it would hurt like hell.

"That man is a lunatic!" Nate yelled, pointing at me. "He killed my brother! He's a fucking killer…oh my god, oh my god!" Nate went into full-on hysterics, but I wasn't listening to him.

"This man needs an ambulance," one of the cops said, kneeling over Eric.

"This isn't what it looks like," Sawyer said, coming forward. "We're the good guys."

"This guy's on the job!" Another cop yelled, pulling some kind of badge out of Eric's pocket.

Several cops turned and pointed their weapons at me as I tried to sit up.

I lifted my hands in surrender. "I am unarmed," I said quietly.

"You're under arrest," another policeman said, pulling out handcuffs and snapping them on my wrists.

"What the fuck?!" Sawyer stepped forward, arguing with the cops, but I barely heard them.

"Lawyer's already on the way to the police station!" Boone called after me as a cop led me outside.

"Don't say anything until we get there!" Sawyer yelled, following us.

I barely heard them, though.

Getting arrested was the least of my worries.

The only thing I could think about was Lucy.

She'd seen the beast beneath my polished exterior.

Now she knew firsthand who I really was.

So I'd saved her.

But I'd also lost her.

The last thing I saw as they put me in one of the police cars was Lucy's devastated, tear-filled face. And she couldn't even look at me.

CHAPTER TWENTY-NINE

Lucy

"WELL?" I asked Sawyer the moment he was off the phone.

"I mean…it's not great. Wes's attorney isn't a criminal defense guy, but he recommended someone and is trying to reach him now."

I knew all the legal stuff was a big deal, but I couldn't bring myself to worry about it right now. All I cared about was Kon's state of mind. How was he? Was he in an overcrowded cell? Was he terrified about what was going to happen because of all of this?

I sure as hell was. Kon had risked not just his life, but also his career and his reputation, to save me from my psychotic ex-boyfriend. I'd never intended to drag him into all of this, and now he was at the center of it.

"When can we see him?" I asked Sawyer, walking over to the coffeepot to brew another pot.

"They said visiting hours are Tuesday and Thursday, but he has to have a bond hearing and get processed before he's eligible."

A fresh round of tears sprung to my eyes at the mention of "visiting hours" and "bond hearing." Kon was a prisoner, all because Nate was a greedy criminal.

"Lucy, stop," Sawyer said firmly. "You're already shaky from the amount of coffee you've had. You don't need any more."

I dropped the scoop back into the coffee grounds and turned to face him, tears streaming down my face.

"I don't know what else to do, Sawyer. I need something to do. This waiting is too much."

He nodded. "I could start drinking again, and you could join me."

My jaw dropped, but before I could get any words out, he was laughing.

"Kidding," he said. "But yeah, all of this…it's a lot."

"Eric is still alive, though, right?"

When the paramedics had arrived at the warehouse, they'd loaded Eric onto a stretcher and rushed him to the hospital. Though he'd been bloodied beyond recognition, he'd been alive, and for Kon's sake, we needed him to stay that way.

"As far as I know; no one's told me otherwise," Sawyer said. "You need to lie down, Lucy."

The doctor at the hospital had told me the same thing. After I'd been checked over and had photos taken of my injuries, a nurse had brought me some medicine and the doctor had said I'd need to take it easy for at least the next few days.

Taking it easy was impossible, though. How could I relax when the man I was falling in love with was in a jail cell? All I had to do was picture him there and I burst into tears.

"I don't suppose they'd let me drop off some cookies for him," I said, not really joking.

"Probably not."

I sighed heavily. "I'm going to prep some casseroles. I have to do something."

"Luce, you need to get off your feet."

I opened a cookbook app on my phone. "This is a healthy coping mechanism. I have to keep my mind busy."

I was scrolling through recipes, and as soon as I

landed on one for chicken and dumplings—Kon's favorite—I burst into tears again.

"This is crazy," I said, burying my face in my hands. "He was there to save me from a bunch of criminals with guns. Why is he the one in jail?"

————

A COUPLE OF DAYS LATER, the tables had turned.

Kon was out of jail and hadn't been charged with anything. The police and prosecutor's office were still reviewing things, but once the Mavericks owner had gotten wind of what was going on and sent in a high-dollar defense team, things had started moving quickly.

Eric was alive and stable. Though his nose would probably never look the same, he was expected to make a full recovery. And when he was well enough, he'd be going to jail.

Nate and the men he'd hired were already in jail, and they would be headed to prison from there. We'd gotten a very lucky break when the police discovered the abandoned warehouse had working security cameras, and the footage had been damning for them.

I wasn't crying around the clock anymore, but now I had a new problem.

"What did he say?" I asked Sawyer as soon as he walked into the house.

He'd gone over to Kon's house, and since Kon wasn't responding to any of my calls or texts, it had been hell when Sawyer had left me behind.

"He's Kon, so…he didn't say a whole lot," Sawyer said.

"Don't play games with me," I said. "Whatever he said about me, I want to know."

My brother met my gaze, sympathy swimming in his eyes.

"It's too much, isn't it?" I said, my voice catching with emotion. "He doesn't want to be with someone who has a psycho ex he ends up in jail over."

"Let's go sit down in the family room," he said, grabbing a bottle of water from the refrigerator.

Wondering whether Kon was going to prison had made me physically sick, and I was relieved he was okay on that front, but I'd traded one set of problems for another.

Not only was he not speaking to me, but there was a swarm of reporters camped outside of Sawyer's house. Now that the story about Kon saving his teammate's sister from her kidnappers had broken, every media outlet imaginable wanted to interview me. The security guards Sawyer had hired were making me stay inside the house at all times.

No working at the bakery, no running errands, and worst of all—no going over to Kon's apartment.

"It's not that," Sawyer said once we were seated in the family room. "It's actually the opposite of that."

"Stop being so cryptic," I snapped. "Tell me what he said."

"He said you're too good for him. That you deserve a man who can protect you but also has restraint."

I furrowed my brow, confused. "Restraint? With the men who kidnapped me and could have shot me at any moment?"

My brother scrubbed his hands down his face. "Luce, this stuff is complicated. If Kon had been some average guy, the cops and prosecutor probably would have charged him with something. We all could have been charged. We should have let the cops handle it, but...Kon and I just couldn't. Wouldn't, I guess. Our team owner's money and clout got us out of this."

"As long as you're out of it, that's all that matters."

He gave me a serious look. "We have to be on our best behavior for the next decade or so. We're damn lucky Rosa Romano values us enough to get us out of this mess and keep us around. Beating people within an inch of their life is bad for PR."

I looked at the ground, feeling defeated. "None of this would have happened if I hadn't come here."

"Yeah, and I'd be passed out on that couch you're sitting on, putting away a case of beer a day. And Kon wouldn't have any idea what it's like to have a relationship with a good person, who doesn't steal his money and cheat on him."

I wrapped my arms around myself, thinking about what he'd said.

"You're the only woman he's been with besides Svetlana," Sawyer said. "I mean, for more than one night. And the fact that he thinks you'd be better off without him and you think he'd be better off without you is just proof of how fucked up you both are. You both have exes who did this to you."

My brother had gone from dazed and drunk to being the voice of reason. He was right, of course. Nate was in jail and I no longer had to live in fear. Svetlana was in another country and Kon was finally free of her. The hard parts were over.

So why were we not together right now?

"How do we fix it?" I said softly. "Or at least, how do I fix what's going on with me?"

"You stay. You've got no reason to leave now, so you stay and give Kon a little time to come to his fucking senses. You remind him what his life was like before you. Trust me, it sucked. That fucker was lonely. And you stop feeling so damn guilty all the time."

My brother's words hit close to home, for more than one reason.

"Do you ever feel guilty?" I asked him.

His shoulders sank. "Yeah. The guilt started when Annie got sick. I thought all the time about how it should have been me." His eyes shone with unshed tears. "She didn't deserve to suffer like that."

I remembered the first time I met the beautiful, vibrant woman who would become my sister-in-law. Everything about Annie was good, and she was grateful for the small things in life. She'd loved Sawyer for his heart, not for his money and fame.

"No, she didn't," I said.

"She wanted me to keep going," he said, wiping the tears from the corners of his eyes. "Life doesn't give us unlimited chances. She used to say that all the time. I've seen the way you and Kon look at each other, and I know what you've both been through to get here."

It was strange, looking at both the little boy who had dumped sand in my hair in our sandbox, and the man who had fought through his grief to give life another go.

"I'm really proud of you," I said. "For so many reasons."

He smiled. "I'm proud of you, too, sis. Now let's try a boring, predictable life for at least a little while, okay?"

I laughed. "Yeah. Okay."

My heart wasn't in it, though.

Everything inside of me screamed that Kon needed me. Just as I needed him.

Beneath that gruff, tattooed exterior was a gentle, sensitive man. Sawyer and his teammates probably would have burst out laughing if I said that out loud —but they weren't intimate with him. They didn't look in his eyes when he was inside of them, baring his soul in a way I'd never thought possible with any man. Much less a guy like Kon. They didn't know the broken man beneath like I did. And that man fucking needed me.

Sawyer was distracted doing something on his phone, so I pulled out mine thoughtfully.

Kon would never make the first move if he thought I was too good for him or whatever bullshit was going on in his head. So it had to be me, despite my own similar thoughts.

Because I loved him. I wasn't falling for him anymore. I was already head over heels. I'd sensed it before everything went to hell, but the moment I'd seen him hiding behind that dumpster, ready to save me? I'd known he was it for me.

Now it was just a matter of convincing him to give us a chance.

Lucy: Hey. I wanted to check on you, make sure you're okay. And I never had a chance to thank you. Will you call me? Please? I have something I need to get off my chest.

CHAPTER THIRTY

Kon

I SLEPT for sixteen hours after finally being released from jail.

Jail.

It had been a strange experience for me. One I never wanted to repeat. I'd been willing to do whatever it took to save Lucy, but I would have been a liar if I hadn't felt like someone was choking me while I'd been behind bars. I wasn't generally claustrophobic, but knowing I couldn't leave? That had fucked with my head big time.

I'd been in jail before. Arrested twice for minor teenage infractions, shoplifting and breaking and entering, but this had been different. As a kid who'd been starving, I'd been full of hate and bravado and misplaced determination. I'd had nothing to lose, after all. As a grown man who made millions of dollars and had a very exclusive life, I had fucking everything to lose.

Luckily, my teammates and then the owner of the Mavericks had gotten involved, so I'd been out faster than I would have thought. Charges had been dropped, the truth had come out, and from what the lawyers had told me, everything was going to be okay. Rosa Romano, who owned the Mavericks, had said she wanted to meet with the four of us who'd gone to get Lucy, so I figured we were going to get some kind of lecture. But that was okay. She'd saved my ass and I'd take whatever lecture or fine or anything else she chose to dish out. My only concern was that she would try to trade me. I really didn't want to go anywhere else after all of this. The Mavericks were more than just teammates; they'd become my family.

That meeting wasn't for a few more days, though, and Coach Gizzard had told me to take a few days off to decompress before coming back to work. The team was on a road trip for a few more days anyway, so I didn't have anywhere to be until the day after tomorrow, which was why I was restless as hell today. I'd already worked out in my building's gym, ordered groceries, talked to my grandmother, and checked in with Wes. Now there was nothing.

It was strange how lonely it felt to be this separated from everything I loved.

Hockey.

My teammates.

Lucy.

Fuck, I missed Lucy more than I wanted to admit.

I'd used the word "love" when I'd been with Svetlana because it was expected. We were a couple. We lived together, slept together, and planned to be together forever. I'd said it because it seemed oddly rude not to. But I hadn't felt it. I just hadn't known it at the time. I'd thought pleasant and comfortable was what love was.

Now that I'd actually fallen in love with someone, I realized how wrong I'd been.

Romantic love was something else entirely.

Lucy had become my reason for smiling every day.

My reason for breathing.

I'd been alive before, and I'd continue to be a functional human being going forward, but it wasn't the same as truly living. And I didn't know how to come to terms with losing the best thing I'd ever had, even if it was for the best.

When my phone buzzed with a text from Lucy, my heart momentarily skipped a beat. Until I remembered how we'd gotten to this point.

Eric's bloody face haunted my dreams.

Not because I felt guilt or regret, but because Lucy had seen me do it.

She had to be horrified she'd ever let a man like me touch her.

It didn't seem fair that she wanted to say whatever was on her mind in person, but I'd let her if it was important to her. Just not yet.

I was still a little shell-shocked after everything that happened.

My phone buzzed again and I looked down to see a group text from a handful of my teammates.

Boone: This road trip is so lame without you, Kon. You comin' back to work anytime soon?

Rory: You're not missing anything—we have a curfew. Coach grounded the whole team. Said we weren't to be trusted.

Wes: Which is hilarious considering all the shit you guys do that he doesn't know about...

Rory: Who, me? I'm a fucking angel. What are you talking about?

Boone: Kon! Where the fuck are you? Hellooo?

I sighed, shaking my head as I tried to formulate a response.

Kon: I just got done working out. What are you assholes doing other than harassing me?

Boone: On a flight to Detroit. Then home tomorrow.

Kon: I'll be at practice the following day.

Wes: Thank god. I don't think Sanders knows what to do starting three games in a row. He's a nervous wreck.

Kon: He's young, but very talented. He'll be fine. Give him a chance.

We talked for a few more minutes before I finally told them I had to shower, even though that was a lie. I had nowhere to go and nothing to do.

And it really fucking sucked.

I'D JUST GOTTEN BACK from the gym the next morning when someone knocked on the door. The media had been camped out near my building for several days, waiting for a chance to talk to me, so only people who knew the code could get in. Sawyer knew it, of course, but he'd just been here yesterday, and my other friends like Boone and Rory were out of town.

I peered through the peephole and blew out a breath.

Lucy.

She knocked again, more impatiently this time

and I slowly turned the dead bolt and opened the door.

"Lucy." I wasn't sure what to say or do, so I just stood there.

"You and I have to talk," she said, looking up at me with annoyance in her eyes.

"I'm sorry. I just thought it best for us to have a little time to—"

"To what?" she demanded, brushing past me. "Wallow in self-pity?"

"I do not understand wallow."

"To feel sorry for yourself. Is that what you're doing here?" She made a sweeping motion with her hand as I closed the door behind us. The last thing I needed was for the neighbors to hear anything.

"I'm not doing anything," I said, watching in confusion as she paced around my living room.

"I know you've been through a lot in your life," she said, looking up at me, her blue eyes fixed on me intently. "And getting arrested probably didn't help with your demons, but I thought we had something special."

"We did, but—" I began.

"Why is there a *but*? Did we or didn't we? Yes or no?"

"Yes." I frowned, unsure where she was going with this.

"What did you do when Dmitri did what he did to Svetlana?"

"What?"

"Konstantin Volkov. Pay attention." She walked up to me and poked her finger in my chest. "What did you do when that horrible man took your friend?"

"I found her."

"And then?"

"I...killed him."

"Because he was a vile man who did something really awful to an innocent young woman."

I could only nod. I wasn't sure what else to do.

"And I already knew this, right? You told me what you did to him. In great detail, if I recall."

"Yes." I looked down to where she still had a finger in my chest, wondering where she was going with this.

"Konstantin. I fell in love with you *anyway*. So why would you think that doing the same thing for me would somehow change things?"

We stood there for what seemed like a long time, just a few inches apart, her bright blue eyes burning into mine.

She'd fallen in love with me.

This gorgeous, smart, sexy, amazing woman loved me.

Still.

"Lucy." I reached out and gently brushed her hair back off her shoulder, so I could rest my hand on the side of her neck. Her eyes fluttered closed for a moment, though she didn't move otherwise. "You are…" I couldn't articulate what I needed to say in English, so I said it in Russian. "The most resplendent woman I've ever met. You make me whole. You brought me to life. I can't imagine going forward without you, but I also can't imagine mixing my darkness with your light."

She frowned. "You know I didn't understand a word of that."

I nodded, shaking my head. "It is difficult to say those words in English. What you are to me…what you've come to mean to me is not easy to translate."

"There's a really easy phrase you can use," she whispered.

Oh, hell.

She wanted me to tell her that I loved her.

And I wanted to. More than anything.

"Lucy." I pulled her closer, so her body was resting against mine. "I know what you want. What you need. But it's not me. Don't you see what I am?"

"I do." She rested her cheek against my chest. "I see exactly who you are. The man who came for me, putting himself at great personal risk. The man who would have killed for me. The man who got arrested protecting me. The strongest, bravest man I've ever known."

I wrapped my arms around her, holding her tight as I squeezed my eyes shut. I loved this woman more than anything or anyone. It gutted me that she'd seen me lose control. How could she want to be with a man who could turn violent like that? I didn't understand it, and more than that, I didn't want it for her. She deserved better.

"My love…" I kissed the top of her head.

"So you do love me!" She didn't move but her voice was laced with humor.

"Of course." I reached out to lift her chin with two fingers. "Since the first time I kissed you."

She smiled tremulously. "Me too."

"But…" I took a deep breath. "I am not what you need. You need someone you aren't afraid of. Someone who will fill your life with light and happiness and all the wonderful things you deserve. Me, I am darkness. Violence. Brutality."

"Seriously?" She took a step back, shaking her head. "Let's see if I can address that nonsense you just spouted. Darkness? That would be a woman who caught her boyfriend doing something both illegal and immoral, and instead of fighting for what was right, she ran away and hid. Violence? That would be having an ex who sends thugs to beat you up and instead beat up on a couple of elderly men you befriended. Brutality? How about being kidnapped, tied up, beaten, and traumatized by your ex and his friends? I just faced all that! How's that for dating a man that I'm not, in fact, afraid of?" She glared at me.

"What are you saying, Lucy?" I asked slowly. She'd never looked more beautiful than she did right now, her chest heaving and her blue eyes brighter than I'd ever seen them. God, I loved this woman. How could I keep trying to push her away?

"You're exasperating," she said in a voice laced with frustration. "Has anyone ever told you that?"

I grimaced. "I don't know what that means, so maybe?"

Instead of continuing to be annoyed, she laughed. "It means you're maddening and stubborn, but that's not the point."

"What is the point?"

"That I love you. That I think you love me too. And together, we can cancel out all that darkness until there's light again."

Once again, we stared at each other.

"You are not…afraid of me?"

"Afraid of you? The only time I'm truly not afraid is when I'm with you."

"What happens if one day we decide to have children? What if they see who I am?" It nearly broke me to say that out loud.

"I hope they do," she whispered. "I can only dream of having a little boy who's strong and gentle and kind while simultaneously protective and loving. Just like his father."

Tears stung my eyes.

No one had ever talked about me being a father. Much less a good one. A loving one.

I didn't even remember my own, so I'd always figured I wouldn't have any kids.

And once again, Lucy was changing everything I thought I knew about myself.

"Lucy. Sweetheart." I blindly reached for her, tugging her against my chest as a dam of emotion seemed to burst out of me.

I couldn't remember the last time I'd cried.

Hell, I couldn't remember the last time I cared about something enough to cry.

I'd cry for Lucy, though.

I'd do anything for her.

CHAPTER THIRTY-ONE

Lucy

I HELD on to Kon for all I was worth, still afraid he could slip away from me at any moment.

"You aren't leaving," he said, kissing my temple.

It was a statement, not a question. But I understood because I felt the same way about him. I'd come over here to tell him he wasn't giving up on us, not to ask him not to, so I couldn't blame him for doing the same with me.

"No," I said softly.

"But if I get traded and I have to leave..." He cleared the emotion from his throat. "Will you come with me?"

Vulnerability swirled in his dark eyes. How could

anyone think this man was stoic? Now that I loved him, I saw Kon for who he truly was—a man who felt deeply, even if it was hard for him to express it sometimes.

I stepped back slightly, making sure he could see my eyes as I responded. "Yes. If you get traded to Florida, California, or even New Zealand, I'm going with you."

He smiled. "New Zealand?"

"That's right."

He kissed me, his lips brushing over mine gently, like he was afraid of hurting me. I wrapped my arms around his neck and pressed my body against his, eliciting a groan.

"Lucy…" he said, his breath warm on my lips. "Your soft, sweet body is mine now. All mine. I will never want to leave the bed."

I hummed with amusement. "An intriguing idea, but you'd get sick of banging me if you did it around the clock."

His grin was devilish. "Not for a very long time, my love."

I couldn't get enough of his tender, affectionate side. There was another side I wanted more right now, though. Tugging at the sides of his shirt, I worked it up until he got the hint and pulled it up and over his head.

This time, my gaze didn't see the defined cuts of muscle in the same way. I saw the ink overlaying each ripple and my heart broke for the young man who had fought for his own survival. Life hadn't been fair to him, but he wasn't bitter.

Trailing my fingertips over his chest, I paused on a jagged, faded scar.

"Just a little stab wound," he said, not even needing to look to see where my hand was.

My eyes clouded with tears. "I wish I could have loved you then."

He took my hand and kissed my fingers. "I was not the same person then. I had to walk through the fire to get here."

"Never apologize for who you are or what you've done." My voice broke as tears flowed down my cheeks. "You are a fierce survivor and protector. I wouldn't change a single thing about you."

His eyes shone as he cupped my face in his hands. "You are my angel, Lucy. I would walk through the fire a thousand times to get to you."

My hands went to his sweats, which I pushed down as our mouths crashed together. We both kicked off our shoes and somehow, he managed to get my clothes off with hardly a break from kissing me.

I'd never been with a man who brought the frenzied desire out of me that Kon did. As he carried me to his bedroom, I burned for him.

He put me on his bed and wasted no time putting on a condom. Foreplay was good, but not this time. This time, we both needed our connection immediately.

I cried out as he buried himself deep inside me, his lips hovering over mine.

"I will never let you down, my Lucy," he said softly. "I will take care of you forever."

I stroked a hand over his hair. "I know. And I'll take care of you, too."

He didn't waste time going slow. Every stroke was deep and hard, a primal sealing of our promises to each other. I clung to him, my body wrapped around his as we both climbed closer to release.

When he hooked his arm around my leg and pushed it up toward my chest, he found a spot that brought me to the edge almost immediately.

"Oh my god, I'm going"

I couldn't finish the sentence with words. Instead, it was a deep, desperate cry of satisfaction as I splintered into a thousand pieces. He was close behind me, groaning as he climaxed and then resting his forehead on mine.

"That was..." I closed my eyes and took a few

breaths, still not able to wrap my mind around it. "Incredible doesn't really do it justice."

He moved to my side, taking my hand and kissing my fingers as he said something in Russian.

"What did you say?" I asked him.

"That you are my light."

I snuggled against him, feeling perfectly content for the first time in my life. There was nothing I wanted or needed that I didn't have. The fears I'd had about losing him were gone. Kon and I had just pledged ourselves to one another with our bodies in a way words couldn't.

I didn't know what the future held, but whatever it was—joy or pain, highs or lows—I knew we'd face it together.

EPILOGUE

Kon

Two months later

"I don't understand," I told Lucy as we walked up to Nash's house carrying what felt like a hundred packages. "I thought baby showers were for women?"

"That's old school," she replied, opening the front door and calling out to Sariah.

"Hi!" Nash's now fiancée stepped out from the kitchen with a grin. "You've got the envelopes?"

"Of course." Lucy wiggled her purse, indicating she had whatever Sariah was talking about.

"I'm so excited," Sariah said. "I can't wait to find out what they're having."

"Do you know?" I asked, putting down the packages I'd been carrying.

Sariah frowned. "You really didn't tell him?"

"Are you crazy?" Lucy laughed. "The way these guys talk on road trips? None of them can be trusted to keep a secret this big!"

"You don't trust me?" I asked, though I knew she was joking and was only referring to this top-secret surprise baby shower. I was very confused but Lucy had told me to be patient and I'd find out when the others did.

"With my life," Lucy said, her eyes twinkling. "Just not with the sexes of our friends' babies."

Lucy and Sariah dissolved into gales of laughter, leaving me shaking my head.

I didn't care what was going on as long as Lucy was happy. She'd been having a blast helping Sariah plan Hadley and Sheridan's joint gender-reveal party. The twist was that on top of the party, they were also planning a surprise shower and I didn't understand how it was supposed to work since everyone already knew about the party. From what I'd been told, Sheridan and Hadley didn't know there was going to be a shower, since both of them had said they didn't need anything. Sariah and Lucy had decided it was more about the camaraderie and bonding than gifts, so they'd planned this massive surprise anyway. Honestly, I loved watching Lucy fit right in with my Mavericks family.

"Hey, you want a beer?" Nash called to me, holding one up.

"Thanks." I reached for it and joined him in the kitchen as Sariah and Lucy disappeared.

"Hell of a way to spend a day off, huh?" he asked as he pulled a tray of marinated kebabs out of the fridge.

"It's okay." I shrugged. "If the ladies are happy, our lives are better."

Nash met my eye with a grin. "You're not wrong."

"Have you and Sariah set a date?" I asked him since he'd proposed over the holidays.

"Looks like late July."

"I'm happy for you."

"You'll be in the wedding party, right?"

"Whatever you need," I said, nodding.

"It's going to be…*huge*."

I wrinkled my nose. "Really?"

"Sariah's mom and sisters are all over it, and as long as she doesn't have to plan it, Sariah doesn't care enough to argue with her family about it. It's a big deal to them. My mom's pretty excited too. So both moms and the sisters are planning it, her dad and I are paying for it, and Sariah just has to show up."

"This sounds like a fair compromise."

"That was my thought too." He cocked his head. "What about you and Lucy? Going that direction?"

"Whenever she is ready," I said quietly. Lucy had moved in after Christmas and things were going well. "Now we're looking for a house. Maybe a wedding the following year. Whatever she wants."

"I seriously want to give you shit about how pussy-whipped you are," Nash said, dropping his voice and glancing around. "But I'm in the same boat. It's fucking weird to be so happy because of them."

We both grimaced.

Then we laughed.

Life was great.

———

"We didn't need a shower," Sheridan said for what had to be the fifth time. She and Hadley had been equal parts embarrassed and overwhelmed with emotion when they realized what was happening.

"You guys are the best friends ever!" Hadley sniffled, dabbing her eyes with a tissue.

"That's what friends are for," Sariah told her.

"Okay, time for the fun stuff." Lucy rubbed her hands together. "We need Lars and Sheridan and Wes and Hadley on the patio and everyone else out in the yard."

Everyone made their way outside as the two couples stood on the patio together watching the rest of us gather. I felt a jolt of envy seeing my friends with their pregnant wives. Both women were glowing, something I'd thought was just bullshit you said to a pregnant woman to make her feel better about weight gain and such. In this case, it was absolutely the truth. Even stoic, overly serious Lars had a huge smile on his face as Sheridan leaned against him.

For the first time in my life, I wanted to be a father too. The thought came out of nowhere but I had no time to think about it because Lucy was holding what looked like four thick, long cylinders. I assumed they were going to shoot colored glitter or something, since I'd seen this on TV.

"So here's the deal," Sariah said. "Everyone placed bets earlier as to what sex the baby of each couple is. But that was just a distraction because here's the real surprise…" She turned to Lucy.

"There are *three* babies in the mix." Lucy smirked.

Silence fell over the crowd.

"That's not fair," Boone muttered. "So we all lost?"

"I don't understand," I said loudly, since I always had issues with language anyway and everyone expected me to be the one to ask questions.

"It means one of the couples is having…" Sariah began.

"Twins!" Lucy finished excitedly.

There was a flurry of conversation and laughter as people tried to figure out which couple it was. Lars, Sheridan, Wes, and Hadley didn't give anything away, though, merely standing there patiently.

Essentially, both women had gotten pregnant at the same time. Their due dates were only a week apart and both looked equally pregnant to me. It wasn't like one of them was much larger than the other. Sheridan was a plus-size supermodel, but her body hadn't changed much from what I could see. She simply had a protruding belly now, and it was the same for Hadley. There was no way to tell which of them was carrying twins.

Of course, what did I know? I'd never been friends with anyone who was pregnant before.

"We want everyone to split up into two groups," Sariah said. "Lars and Sheridan will stand on my left, and Wes and Hadley on my right. If you think Lars and Sheridan are having twins, stand on the left side of the yard. If you think it's Wes and Hadley stand on the right."

"But how will the pink or blue smoke or whatever tell us who's having twins?" Boone asked.

"Just be patient," Sariah told him, grinning.

She handed two thick tubes that almost looked like large Roman candles to Lars and Sheridan, and Lucy handed two to Wes and Hadley.

"One of the tubes is empty," Lucy said. "So you'll shoot all four at the same time."

"Are you ready?" Sariah asked.

Everyone in the crowd started to hoot and whistle, calling encouragement to them.

"On the count of three," Lucy said.

"One, two—" She and Sariah counted together.

"Three!" Everyone yelled at the same time and the two couples shot colored smoke into the sky.

Two clouds of pink and one of blue.

Wes and Hadley had one empty cylinder and a cloud of blue smoke.

Meaning Lars and Sheridan were having twin girls.

Holy shit.

Everyone crowded around both couples, playfully chastising Lars and Sheridan for not telling anyone they were having twins and congratulating all of them. I watched from a distance, happy for my friends even as I sought out Lucy.

As if she'd sensed something was up, she moved closer to me.

"You okay?" she asked.

"Do you want children?" I whispered against her ear.

"Yes." She nodded. "Don't you?"

"Yes. Very much."

Her eyes widened. "Oh my god. Are you getting baby fever?"

"I don't know what this means, but yes? I want a baby with you. Maybe several."

"Okay."

"Okay?" I was surprised at the simple answer.

"Not right *now*," she said, tipping up her face as she chuckled. "There needs to be a ring on this finger first, but yes. I want babies too. Before I'm too old to enjoy them."

"Wedding next year, maybe a baby the year after that?"

"Yes." She moved into my arms and I stroked my hands down her back as I kissed her.

"I love you, Lucy."

"I love you too."

"I am ready to go home and start practicing."

"I'm one of the hostesses," she said, shaking her

head. "And the girls have nine thousand gifts to open. Plus, I know you're going to want cake."

"Okay. I will settle for cake. For now."

"Baby-making practice later," she said, playfully elbowing me in the ribs.

"Deal."

I watched as she made her way over to where Sariah, Sheridan, Hadley, and a few other ladies had gathered. With a smile, I wandered over to join my friends and teammates.

"Congratulations," I said to Lars, shaking his hand.

He grinned. "It's been killing me keeping it a secret, but we didn't know the sex and we wanted to wait until today to tell everyone."

"Are they identical or fraternal?" Boone asked him.

"Identical." Lars looked over at Sheridan. "I hope they look like her."

"And another boy for our captain," Nash said. "I think there will be a lot of babies coming in the next few years."

"Anything you want to tell us?" Rory asked him.

"No kids until we're married," he said. "But sure. We want kids when we're ready."

I didn't contribute to the conversation, happy to hang out and listen. At one point, I looked up and found Lucy's gaze on me. I winked and she blew me a kiss.

A cloud of contentment settled over me, something I'd never experienced before, and it was all because of her.

Right here, in a random Missouri neighborhood I'd never heard of until a few years ago, I had everything I'd ever wanted and a few things I'd never allowed myself to even dream of.

Not bad for a skinny kid from Siberia.

WANT MORE?

The next book in the St. Louis Mavericks, Hard Hit, is the story of Michael Boone. It releases March 21, 2023.

ALSO BY BRENDA ROTHERT

Chicago Blaze Series

Book 1 - Anton

Book 2 - Luca

Book 3 - Victor

Book 4 - Knox

Book 5 - Alexei

Book 6 - Easy

Book 7 - Jonah

Book 8 - Kit

Book 9 - Olivier

Sin city saints Series

Book 1 - Maverick

Book 2 - Pike

Book 3 - Pax

St. Lous Mavericks series

Book 1 - Hard Fall

Book 2 - Hard Limit

Book 3 - Hard Pass

Buried

Sweet Sixteen

His

Alpha Mail

Healing Touch

Barely Breathing

Exiled

ABOUT THE AUTHOR

Brenda Rothert lives in Central Illinois with her husband, children and three dogs. She loves to hear from readers through her website or her Facebook Group, Rothert's Readers.

ALSO BY KAT MIZERA

Las Vegas Sidewinders:

Dominic

Cody's Christmas Surprise

Drake

Karl

Anatoli

Zakk

Toli & Tessa

Brock

Vladimir

Royce

Nate

Sidewinders: Ever After

Jared

Dmitri's Christmas Angel

Ian

Dax (*A Royal Protectors/Sidewinders crossover novel*)

Suze's Diary (A Sidewinders Companion Novella)

Sidewinders: Generations:

Zaan

Tore

Anton

Van

Decker

Alaska Blizzard:

Defending Dani

Holding Hailey

Winning Whitney

Losing Laurel

Saving Sara

Chasing Charli

A Very Blizzard Christmas

Tending Tara

Calling Cassie

Playing Peyton

Catching Lana (An Alaska Blizzard Companion Novel)

St. Louis Mavericks (with Brenda Rothert)

Hard Fall

Hard Limit

Hard Pass

Hard Luck

Lauderdale Knights:

Slap Shot

Big Shot

Long Shot

Hot Shot

Sure Shot

Rock Hard:

Play

Pause

Rewind

Fast Forward

The Royal Trilogy:

Nowhere Left to Fall

Nowhere Left to Run

Nowhere Left to Hide

Royal Protectors:

Sandor

Cocky Protector (book 1.5, part of the Cocky Heroes Club series)

Xander

Axel

Dax (*A Royal Protectors/Sidewinders crossover novel*)

Inferno:

Salvation's Inferno

Temptation's Inferno

Redemption's Inferno

Tropical Inferno (formerly "Tropical Ice")

Romancing Europe:

Adonis in Athens

Smitten in Santorini

Lucky in Lugano

View Kat's entire collection of books at
www.KatMizera.com

USA Today Bestselling author Kat Mizera was born in Miami Beach with a healthy dose of wanderlust. She's lived from coast to coast, and everywhere in between, but home is wherever her family is.

A devoted mom and wife to her wonderful and supportive husband (Kevin) and two amazing boys (Nick and Max), Kat loves to travel the globe with her adventurous, hockey loving family. Greece is at the top of that list. She hopes to one day retire there, spending her days writing books on the beach.

Kat is former freelance sports writer who now writes steamy hockey romance about her favorite fictional teams, the Las Vegas Sidewinders and the Alaska Blizzard. The library of novels she's penned also include sexy contemporary stories about base-ball stars, alpha sex club owners, special forces heroes, rock stars and royalty. Regardless of genre, her books about bad boys with hearts of gold will steal your breath, rock your world and melt your heart.

WHERE TO FOLLOW KAT:

WEBSITE
FACEBOOK
TWITTER
INSTAGRAM
BOOKBUB
KAT'S PRIVATE FACEBOOK GROUP